THE
COALS
OF
FIRE

MERENPTAH ASANTE

Copyright © 2023 by Merenptah Asante

Paperback: 978-1-960861-32-0
eBook: 978-1-960861-31-3
Library of Congress Control Number: 2023909765

This is a work of fiction.

Table of Contents

Chapter One

Ascension Sunday. The new canvas of Obatala's Day filled the sky with bright and dazzling lights. The night before, stars shot across the sky, meteors fell into the sea, new gorges broke the land, and wild men dropped out of the skies and vanished without trace. The night was tranquil, and the lights soon faded into the vast and limitless solar system.

But at daybreak the dawn rose with a burning red sun. The dawn dripped and dripped, and dripped bright - scarlet - red - blood, before the clouds smeared and the horizon bled with a kaleidoscope of colours. Colours that ran as in a revolving washing machine of mixed clothes where colours ran into each other, until the clouds became anarchic fabrics of light: fiery reds, blues, oranges, and whites. The brush strokes of the immortal and Almighty mind of Obatala's consort the blind Oduduwa, coupled with the creator of the world. But her serenity that in the before - day promised a bright and a beautiful day with no genesis of chaos; no hints of hurricanes, high seas, nor billows that rolled on the bay. Not a single hint of secretive powerful forces that will come smashing the rocks and flooding the land; nothing like this drastic change.

In the shrines of Yemaya, the cow's liver was cut, dissected, divined. The divinations read trouble. The amulets told of lands far off and strangers of powerful magic that would encroach, enclose the land, and banish the inhabitants from the groves of their ancestors forever. That the very children will be lost in their own homes, and that some shall become victims of their own indoctrination and preach disturbing dreams like pastors of turbulence.

The ngomas everywhere in their various divinations spoke the same truths with one accord. This land rising out of the silver sea that rides the waves as if it were a giant bird with flight of wings. This once impregnable wall carved by the coarse hands of warriors, consecrated by the spirits of flying spears thrown into the sky with unimaginable might. These fortresses of stone that would crumble like the statue of Ozymandias. Once noble, but now, head bowed in shame. This triple Kingdom will fall. This land, once amaranthine would die. The hazel eyes of its children would smoulder and burn like diamonds in coals of fire.

Out on the ceaseless sea, in the twinkling of an eye the climate changed. Murmurs in the factory of human cargo as the ships raised anchor and headed off the coast of Africa. Days after above the sea, thunder clapped, lightning flashed and forked, and rain came; dropped, sweeping across the morning sky like carpets of blanket weed. On the sea, Desire rocked, rolled, and heaved at the bow. The winds cardinal and vengeful tossing her like a boy's toy sailboat of coconut shell, runaway and forlorn against the horizon, engulfed by the shy rays of the setting sun and castaway on the cliff of the water mark, over the angry, and turbulent waves of the Caribbean Sea. The thunderstorm crashed, and the wind moved upon the water, crushing the rocks, and bashing the waves of the Spanish Main.

Coursing through the mouth of the storm, the filed and jagged teeth of the wind, Desire was feeble as the storm chewed her sails, slicing them like wafers of cooked meat. At the helm of the hurricane the wind howled, the sea as if threatening to give up its dead broke the clashing rocks into splinters of granite; opened its throat, vomited, and regurgitated shells, dead sea and river fishes, multiple human limbs; other body parts: heads, feet, torsos, single human limbs that floated like crabs' legs; ambergris, dead and dry driftwood, wood retched from the wretched and exploding gut of the rough and explosive sea.

The sea made drawing, scratching, scraping sounds as it threw each wave inshore and drew them back again, pulling the debris, pebbles, and shale, back from the shore as the waves withdrew and re-entered the sea. It ate and regurgitated as the Romans digested and ingested their food. This was indicative that it was that time in the world when might was right, and the only truth was pomp, power, and empire. It was an unfortunate time for those like us without seafaring nations. A chattel's labour was free; it mattered little how hard they worked. Everyone agreed they contributed nothing to the world. And they believed it, too. They believed that they were dumb, black beasts, that they were worthless, as divined by the clerics in the graveyards of the sea.

So many ships had passed this way before: some bound for the Carolinas, the Caribbean islands, Melanesia, East, West, South and North Africa, the African Islands; others for Brazil, South, Central and North America; the far East, Southeast Asia, Australasia: blackbirding; ferrying men, women, and children into fields of cotton, rice, bananas, tobacco, indigo and sugar cane; carrying them off into bondage; into buck breaking, anal brothels. But mostly, the young, out of Africa. It seemed to me then, looking back at the dimmed past that all nations of the earth like mammoth - flesh - eating - leeches fed on the black - body - broken, prostituted, objectified, and sodomized.

Again, Desire rocked, rolled, and heaved on in midship; her body limbering to break into two pieces, like the judgment of Gomorrah for her sins, the cries of the sinful sinners of the soul sickened city rose with each heave of the waves that splashed high as four storey houses. The sea tore open ropes made of hemp and sizzle rolled into tubes hard as iron into shreds like tissues, tender as flesh, munching them like clans of laughing hyenas tearing carcases scavenged from a kill on the Sarangeti; growling and barking gluttony as they dragged the day's dinner into the flying dust, tearing it into pieces like slices of bacon; dragging and tearing a devoured prey, scavenged from the dungle of corpses on the hill.

The slavers lashed by the wrath of the sea and the howling tsunami of the wind, ran from bow to stern and back again as the ship threw from side to side, now entering the belly of the storm. The captain through his spyglass watched every wave mounting. Shouting at the slave sailors as buckets and barrels bailed water from the decks, pulled on his pipe with the nonchalance of a well-travelled, weathered seafarer.

He picked his nose with his thumb, retrieving a hidden pearl of dried snot hiding in the recesses of his right nostril; hooked another from the left and flicked them both into the sea. Took the pipe from his mouth and handed it to the naked white child standing at his side; spat into the sea and dug dry mucus out of the corners of his eyes, wiping his hands in his clothes. He was confident that the storm would pass. He had seen others; he had seen worse.

Caught in a maelstrom, the ship circled, trapped in a whirlpool. From the holds below the water mark, stark voices of the kidnapped herd; were heard wailing, rose, and fell with the undulation of the swollen rows of waves. On the sea the wind bringing rain and the swelter of the entire ocean. The hurricane with its fangs like a vampire bit into the bow of the ship like a cutlass slicing the jugular veins in the neck of a goat or a human sacrifice, emptying its blood, draining its life force. All on board were objects to the wind, likely to be jettisoned in the shipwreck like boxes thrown overboard, floating, and sinking into the watery grave that is the sea.

Desire heaved at the bow. Rode down the streams of life-threatening waves, lashed by the sea. Sinkable! A barque, the middle masts toppled and crashed as the inferno hopped from bow to stern. Smoke engulfing the deck. On the wind the raw scent of blood; the stench of human excrement and burning flesh circled from the holds and inshore. These ships escorted by a shiver of sharks and batteries of barracudas, eating the dead thrown overboard. In the rancour, the howls and whimper of the weeping, frightened cargo, moved not a single sailor to mercy, compassion nor sympathy. These were not people; not humanity, but beasts at worst; at best objects exchangeable for money; items entered ships' logs; cargo. Things passed - on as inheritance, exchange rates, objects like houses put up for mortgages, and paid legal tender for debt.

While she swayed, surged, and rolled forward; vessel that she was rocking into the bay of hell. The crashing timber and falling canvas dropped to the deck with a thunderous, tremulous thud that echoed so loudly that it drowned out the gnashing - wind - ravaged waves of the sea that lashed the hull of the ship with vengeful bitterness for nature was angry. The sailors having substituted rum for the opium of Odysseus's argonauts, staggered into history on the one hand, and on the other hand, heaved buckets and barrels of water out of the sea, scattering the precious liquid onto the ship, scuttling its wastage in panic. They needed every hand on deck but could not risk the depletion of profit. They could not risk a revolt.

Suddenly, there was a fire, the sailors dropping buckets into the salty sea to drown the now thundering flames that now threatened to rip through the decks, while in the holds the moaning of the kidnapped cargo of souls rose more on the violent waves.

Yet, too soon, startled, the slashing tongues of the waves overwhelmed the White men and the ship. The stern pointed upwards; the bow dipped and dropped crashing like a giant oil tanker into the sea. The sea sucked it in; the wailing voices, now astounded began to sing. There was consolation: immersion put out the flames, and there was the hush of a mighty noise. The sea swallowed the ship with the hush of death. Then a hush followed, a densely silence!

Moments later, a child rose on the surface of the waves as if carried by invisible hands inshore. They were dolphins. And as I grew, I remembered the hand splashing blue water out on the sea: the call of a man shouting and kicking for help; splashing, hand raised, beckoning for help; voice crying out; voices crying out; a chorus of murmurings from the depths that shook my soul.

That day held sharp, distinct, and frightening memories for me until now. But I have been resolute not to cry. Found lapped inshore between rocks, which is how they found me. The tribes of New Guinea, in the Pacific rim, blonde haired, blue eyed, and black. I was not the first Avatar ever found in water still in swaddling clothes like an embryo ripped from the walls of the uterus, thrown into the sewer of the city, and I was not the last, nor destined to be the last. This soul of mine is a transported essence. It is a migratory bird.

I had no wish to be born. I am a child of exiles. And all that existed back then; to all that transpired and shall transpire in the end. My soul said, "I am a soldier, created of the great replacements when Europe marched across the globe soldiering!"

This current exile and the two exiles before are recurring cycles of the lives that have made me impregnable to fire. All around me is the scent of burning; fire is my hearth stone; fire is my domain. The crimson colour of the burning flame has a similar fascination for me as moths that bake themselves in the lampshade of an electric bulb, so attracted I am as they are to the light of consuming flame. I am The Third World: I am Libya, Iraq, Palestine, and Afghanistan. And I am China rising. I am as much a child of exile as I am of fire; fire is the maker of my world. In my world it is an all-consuming flame: destruction, resurrection, revelation, and judgment. It is giver of life, love, destruction, and death. I am as much a child of evil as I am of good, like the parables of Leviticus. Let me be Shiva; let me be

Shango; let me be Obatala. I shall make war on the builders of empire and become barbarous by deed and by narrative. Let China rise; let Africa rise; let Russia rise. I am Kali, black as the tents of Kader. I am Abiku, the reincarnate Malcolm X, and I march on coals of fire. I am Horus, I am Osiris the first Avatar.

Chaos like a black anarchic heaven is my morning and evening song. Believe me, disorder, trauma, and bloodshed are the peaceful triads. The valleys in which I thrive. I have drunk the blood of Jesus to become intoxicated with his power. Being so, I am certain that I am bound to heavenly glory; having escaped everlasting hell and washed in the blood of Jesus, whose blood I drink as wine, and whose flesh I eat as bread in the supper of my redemption songs.

That August afternoon in Antigua, it was the year 1736, I watched through the gaps in the hut which they did not set on fire and saw the twelve, wild, Black men that burned and looted our lives. The promise of their freedom set them apart to do unspeakable things to children. Setting fire to our huts with no mercy in their hearts. In the burning inferno, thrown into the midst of the flames I scampered and crawled to the other side. Voodoo has made me impregnable to holocausts because my heart is filled with fire as the three that walked in the furnaces of Babylon. That autumn afternoon, the wind singing through the trees, each leaf a tremolo. A three-year-old without hands, I saw men lynched and fried alive. I am no stranger to whips, strangulations, and amputations. For desensitized by history, I need its madness!

But that was not my first baptism by fire. I saw that spring at Capisterre in 1639, men tied to crosses and crucified in sand as dust engulfed their sinuses and lungs, blinded by the coarse grains of the earth their sight eaten by dust. The first Maroons of Sir Thomas Warner. I saw the Carib massacres. All wars are just when waged in the name of Jesus. And I have eaten, consumed, ingested his blood, and digested his flesh. In his name I shall make wars.

As you know it is only perceptions that obscure the true nature of war. Abiku, I am Abiku, the ever-returning child of the same spirit. History's eyes have seen what the sins of the intelligent ones can do. What he that sits atop the food chain can do?

What might in its resplendent power can glorify. The mystery books whose authors have edited pages that were soaked in bloodier tones have written "Beautiful things have been spoken of thee, oh Jerusalem!" "Oh, Washington! "Oh, Paris!". " Oh, London!" "Oh, Rome!" "Oh, Leopold with his bakery of chocolate hands!" Atrocities have been committed before and shall again be committed. And the White man shall say. 'It was necessary. It was progress. It was legal. His laws made it legal!' The tyranny of David and his domination of the world is just as wars go. I do not lie; I am living witness to his deeds. His crimes against his own and to me, and the tyranny of Naboth to himself and the poverty of his children. For in his book it is written, "Let us go down into the flood and fill this world with rage and hatred. This earth shall rise in blood and coals of fire shall brighten the golden flower of Anarchy. Let us blow up the world and die together. Let us all go down into the flood and end the sun in entropy." Let me explain why we should destroy this temporal world and start anew.

The autumn of 1725 at New York, I saw men cut into pieces; flesh thrown into the Hudson River to feed the fishes; heads and torsos floating in the river of no return. Legs, buttocks, and eyes floated in the red currents of its tides in the watery grave of the river; so many died. We bear no false witness to what he hides and would like to silence but the time has come to speak plainly of his deeds. Truth does not hide forever. And, yet for me, I judge nothing. Lobsters have free will. They devour their own kind. It is part of the human condition. And I, too, shall learn to kill. Cut down the twitching corpse whose hands pull at the noose around his neck, break its arms and hoist it again to the same tree, staining the same leaves. I too shall enclose the land and banish its owners, then have them work their lands for me. Oh, I shall be barbarous, when it is my turn, for vengeance is mine saith the Lord. And if I am the destroyer of worlds. What manner of man shall I become?

Chapter Two

I T WAS MIDDAY. THE SEA was amazingly calm. The men on the decks looked up at the seagulls circling above the white masts of the ships. Albatrosses dipping in the white foam of the ocean. For some the sun was so hot that they shielded their eyes with the palms of their hands as they looked up, so fierce and terrible was the glare of the tropical sun that without this habit they felt that they would go blind. Their eyes roving from sky to sea, marvelled at the lapping, tranquil and azure waves. The English ships sang sea shanties and ballads; emboldened, whores among them danced, frolicked, and flirted with the favourite objects of their cargo of souls. There was a time for merriment of a kind and favourites and targeted were brought up from the holds to exercise; dance, play the banjos and have sex. The sinister plot was that ten percent of the fourteen- to sixteen-year-olds would stand on the auction block impregnated by respective sailors. Higher bids for young single mothers in a bid that paid two for the price of one. Sometimes three. Like the surface of the sea, it seemed harmless fun. But only in a world turned upside down.

As for the kidnapped, for the Spanish sailors, it was a frightening calm. The speed and agility of the English pirates saw them merciless as they played cat and mouse with their bulky, sluggish Don Quote contraptions. For the contestants aboard the ships, this was a game in which there were rules and no rules for each made and played by their own. And how else when humanity was lacking. The white men shared disparate portions of a sliced dog which they ate. But the English held the head and relished the game of sailing ships.

The black rocks stood like newly formed islands jutting out of the sea. Most men on this journey for the first time saw the sailing as exciting. It was true that the Americas were an exciting and beautiful part of the world, but its horrors were gruesome. To the heart – hardened, it was just another place, where men lived, played hard, hardened their hearts, traded in black gold, and made money. To others it was a time in the life of the world where men indulged their fancies and realised their fantasies. Whatsoever took your fancy was within your grasp. Most indulged their baser appetites. Most had private slaves that fulfilled the roles of servant, body warmer and concubine. Most operated brothels on board the ship Most dealt in children; others in boys and women, while adult men that were broken and made effeminate. This was especially so on the Spanish galleons that stole out of Cancun.

The Good Ship Jesus, Saviour of Mankind, crossed the smouldering rim of the Gulf that is the simmering sea. Hawkins a hard man, brain, hard - wired for evil, with a will of iron, chased down three limping Spanish galleons from the Gulf of Mexico. Just after tea, the Spanish flotilla was in full view of the stern cannons. However, this was too easy for Sir John Hawkins. He needed to prove a point that would spread fear and loathing in the warfare of tall ships.

Struck from a hundred knots, The Pizarro was taking in water. Its rear once covered in the chase by The Pinta, which soon proved no deterrent for Hawkins who ordered his stoking boys to feed the hungry mouths of the cannon faster, was haemorrhaging water. Gritting his teeth like a mad dog, he bludgeoned, demanded, shouted his commands that the hard sinewy muscled men of Hull swing the sails and speed broadside. The cannon aiming for the centre of the fleet of three ships, pounding the blind side of the enemy. Then tacked west to fool the Spanish that he feared their guns and strategy of boarding. Placed his ship third port and then in a straight line, pushed South by the wind, turned behind the limping armada and steered starboard, all guns blazing, knocking out its resistance from a hundred yards.

Then from fifty yards breaking the mast of the Magdalene the main ship. Before tacking north to beat them to the Azores where they waited with their guns astern to knock them out; steal their cargo and chase the wind back to Bristol for Black Friday auction. The Spaniards knew they were no match for the speed of the English fleets. They were losing control of the Spanish Main.

It was not Montezuma's gold that attracted the English ships on that bright August morning. Though it shone bright and yellow as the sun, there was something else on board that made men like Hawkins risk their own lives and that of his crew. There was black gold on board, held in the holds of the ship. Worth more than all the silver of Montezuma.

Having shattered its broadside in the Bahamas, he knew that it was taking in water. The three had sailed a straight line from Mexico to Cuba where they took on limes, cotton, and tobacco. But zigzagged to avoid the belching English cannons as he moved ship astern and fired into them with devastating effect, causing havoc and panic amongst the crew with the technology of incendiary, the fire boats crashing into their hulls, their men at the bow, flesh sizzling like bacon. Bitumen and tar from the pitch lakes of Trinidad burning the decks like petroleum on the sands of Megiddo.

Three days later and there they were, the three injured ships stumbling into the harbour of Ponta Delgada. Torn and ripped sails substituted rudders. Barely afloat they docked amidst three Portuguese man' o wars. Tired and worn-out Colonel Francisco Gonzalez wiped the dripping beads of sweat from his forehead and patted the firm backside of the fourteen-year-old boy lying beside him. In this game in an age in which you held life and death over them, they were mere property. You did as you wished with them and that was all. Colonel Francisco Gonzalez had a saying that he did not risk his life for others to taste the sweet fruits of his labours which he supplied but never sampled.

The Magdalene was a floating palace that rivalled the pavilions of pope Alexander Borgia. A third of the servants that served him aboard the main ship were young princes and princesses robbed of their royal inheritance, women whom no man in their tribe would ever have approached out of wedlock. But now spoil, and the captain and lieutenant would find greatest pleasure in breaking their will. Young men whose families had griots that could trace their lineage back millions of seasons were now like toys. The horror that was Europe's heart of darkness. Sodomy, abortions, premature births, infant mortality, bile, hunger, famine, and degrading death. Damirifa due, due, due!

It was whilst captain Franco Don Quote and lieutenant Rafael Batista were visiting the floating palace for an orgy that the English fleet crept into Santiago de Cuba and gave them the surprise of their lives. They managed to race back along the ropes to their respective ships, pulled anchor and hurried to sea. The tactic of sea dogs had allowed this. Hawkins knew the habits of the Spanish and lured them into a false sense of comfort. He enjoyed the hunt. He attacked again delivering a barrage when they reached the Bahamas. The English either drank sparingly or could hold their drink better than the Spaniards, always seemed to have the upper hand.

The English seemed to have backed off from the harbour and pulled away. But that was a decoy; the third Portuguese man 'o war had been purchased by Hawkins for seven teals of silver and five bars of gold. The Spaniards had used Indian and African pearl divers at San Salvador and Santiago de Cuba at the start of the industry, but as the English had spoiled the market the once proud divers became redundant. Anxious to practice their skills many became saboteurs for the English. Twenty of such men were deployed just before nightfall. They swam beneath the three Spanish ships digging holes into the rotting undersides, punching, and hammering in turns, making the damage a slow process of covert leaks that would build up by dawn to cause panic and havoc. To affect this Hawkins clandestine squadrons clambered aboard the ships and hid among the barrels of rice, cotton, limes and indigo. They would strike at second light as the sun disperse its rays over the watery plains of the sea.

The following morning as the sun crept over the horizon, Colonel Francisco Gonzalez asleep with the young girl beside him did not stir as Mungo stole into the cabin, stepping lightly. He looked at the child in the enveloping arms of the Colonel and wondered what pleasures could be got from a child whose primary understanding at that stage in life was play. In his Mandingo tribe you only had sexual relations after marriage. And he was unsure whether the white man on board that wore the chain with the cross had married this child to this man, snoring like a hippopotamus expelling water from its gigantic jaws. He realised that he had no time and placing the cloth around the victim's face slit his throat from ear to ear. The same fate befell Commander Don Quote and Rafael Batista on board their respective ships. When Hawkins boarded the Magdalene there was little resistance. Yet he offered to share proceeds of the sale to every man that helped to rescue the coveted cargo. As the Spanish fleet began to sink and Hawkins and his men became fishers of souls. In his is new role as fisher of souls rescued from the sea as revived cargo that exchanged hands, he had succeeded to bury his enemies. As the divers pulled them aboard like hordes of pearls, resuscitated and dusted for auction his cunning had won. Five hundred black men, women, and children were eventually sold at Lisbon, yielding high profit returns of twenty gold bars for his initial investment and a contract for further business. I saw these events with my own eyes; I experienced them in my mind, body, and soul, and I am reviled by them. It is true that I am a slave!

Chapter Three

I AM ABABIO; YOU ARE NOT the only one. I was a child barely twelve years old when I saw my death three days before the Irishman knocked on the door of our cabin and explained that he had no choice. Some of us will be sold to the Danes, others to the Norwegians. Then after we had hugged our goodbyes, his black sonderkommandos picked eighty – eight of us; marched us to the centre of St Johns; strung us up to The Hanging Tree and burned us alive.

The flames rose, the suffocating stench of burning human flesh rose in the rancour of the air; the cabins torched where twenty children; the unnumbered old, those infirmed, those with disabilities died, anonymous and countless others deceased. The chosen heads of the leaders were put on spikes so all could see what fate would befall those that defied their masters. Caution that unless they repented freedom to be washed in the blood of Jesus, the white and only begotten son of God the father, at judgement in an apartheid heaven above and beyond the clouds. That they, too, would die and forever burn in the fires of everlasting hell, which was worse than our predicament. Yes, I watched myself die. I am the resurrected dead! One of the many souls whose bones were thrown, soul drowned at the bottom of the sea.

'Beware of the ones born with the caul they say. Beware the Abiku, beware the returning ones; beware the Abibio. Break the bangle from the wrist; cut the lock from the head, dissuade them not to return, and cover the graves with cow dung, or best, toss them like dogs drowned in the sea. Do not suffer twins to live in this time. Kill them at birth. They are too sacred.'

Tied to the burning trees, and burned alive, we held hands. The rule was that all twins must die. All those that set fire to Coral Bay in 1733, Stono River in 1739, New York in 1741; those stripped naked and reduced to ashes in Antigua in 1736.

At Saint Barthelemy Captain Jon Larsen controlled the first flotilla by an array of flags that sent messages to the nine other captains. One of whom was responsible for the eleven other ships that went around the world, Captain Erik Erickson was second in command. The other ships with delegated commanders fired into the small island, cannons reverberating like thunder; smoke and fire burning the targeted trees, singeing those not in direct fire. The Dutch had not met such a fierce attack before they ventured from the South American mainland: took Curacao from the Spanish and ventured into the open sea of naval warfare that shook the Caribbean. When it came to the Dutch the Scandinavians were merciless. The captured Dutch seamen were for the Arabian and Ottoman markets. The fairer the better.

Today, however, they were establishing their dominance in the South Caribbean. They needed black sex slaves for the Turks, and white slaves for the Arabs.

Turning south to St Johns the Danish ships gave a wide berth to the Swedes hammering the small island with cannons. Theirs was a friendly rivalry that would not be allowed to spill over and sour their relations. To the Scandinavians slavery had been integral to their economies for a thousand years. They specialised in selling Slavs, Latins; they even sold their own. The Swedes knew that there was another uprising in St Croix; another in St Johns.

The Danes were racing to Coral Bay to put down yet another slave rebellion. It was becoming clear to the Scandinavians that black slavery was very unlike their traditional market where white slaves acquiesced to their fate. Arab and Turkish slaves were grateful to be fed and to stay alive. Black slaves either killed themselves or at a drop of a hat swore to avenge their ancestors. They had been at slavery a very long time. And knew there were marked differences. The black people were a warrior race. Once broken, was yet capable of healing itself and fly at the throats of its former masters, there was power innately instilled in that race. So, they treated it as an enterprise in which you only indulged for a specific period. Hence, their attitude remained pragmatic. St Barthelemy was needed as a holding port for slaves of every hue, upon which service the managers in Stockholm imposed a tax. The messier business of the trade was left to others, not the Swedes, the Danes nor the Norwegians. They had factories for people and saw them as goods that brought taxes. Which fast forward you to my more recent past.

Chapter Four

ALL MY FRIENDS ARE LIKE me: shards of glass, brittle children of light, or if you like, hand mirrors that reflect on walls and from mountains, slags of shingles of glass, glass marbles that are bright and pretty that reflect light.

Perhaps this is part of the human condition: brilliant and dark stars we light up the flat earth for a short while. Everything has its season. In coming here, I pictured every precious moment and continuous past tense of the burning desires of my youth before I left my body. But that is so long ago.

It was leading up to Christmas when I came here, this time around. Christmas, days of carols, pleasant and modulated voices on the BBC radio and music that warmed the heart. Papa listened to the shipping forecast every morning and classics every long evening, and I soon learned to expect to hear and love 'Rodrigo's Concerto de Aranjuez for Guitar and Orchestra' and the sublime and ineffable 'Still, Still, Still.'

Pause if you will and close your eyes and picture me a small dark child on board a ship crossing the Atlantic Ocean on so many journeys, on so many lifelines. Imagine this ship has sailed away from islands of sunshine, leaving family and friends waving behind on the quay. Fourteen long days on the cruise of an ocean liner and landing at a dock anywhere. Coming down the gangway of the ship. As I said, a small, small child, in short trousers, blue socks, shiny blue shoes, blue shirt and blue, woollen winter jacket.

Feel with me the gusts of snow, flakes: some falling about me, others rising from the ground, blowing up into my face. Now open your eyes. Can you see me? Can you see a little, dark child?

Why did they bring me here, knowing that I would be a divided soul? I had no idea that I would be coming here. I am a trafficked soul sold into slavery by the people who love me and swore to protect me. Ten years from now; twenty, thirty years from now? What will I be to this land, if not a stranger?

History has been set in motion: forces over which we have no idea. In our marginalized lives we try to grab control. But we are ghosts on runaway ships. We are wind rushes that add tumult to the hurricanes; we are a conquered race. But we have allowed our conquests to rise and then grow. Here then is our narrative: fulfilment of the book. Replacement of the Bible.

Chapter Five

WHAT IF I SHOULD TELL you a story about my life? Would you believe my life? They that have tried to replace me by rubbing every single page out of my life like a palimpsest, I sing my own song, and leave you to yours. Can a story write itself; sad tales rewrite themselves; great atrocities rewrite themselves? People who are censors of taste and once, having pronounced them good, such tales become the new reality. Power is the ultimate tyrant. This is my tale; believe it or not!

Once upon a time on a moonlit starry, starry night when all the clouds were gathered, glistening brightly like platinum steps in the night sky, I saw white and black Jesus, two twins holding hands in the brightly lit northern night sky. They walked amid stars that shone out of the midnight sun and glowed like flowers that bloomed in amber gardens; they floated through emerald passages that led to pathways, stairwells and stairways swirling through the wild, haunting, and beautiful outer of space. The two twins that looked like Jesus became one, changing, rearranging, reverting, and transforming and ended in a form that flowed out of the gleaming starry, starry night sky. The clouds became a sky of rainbows that turned into a maze of colours like images seen through a kaleidoscope.

Suddenly, as if by transubstantiation, I became Anancy: transforming soul that entered the body of a monkey. And I am, suddenly, the new Christ. This is my story of among many other things, shattered mirrors, and shattered dreams. We did not come here to die! I am Abiku.

Once upon a time Adam looked upon the world through a trillion blades of grass until that day when he discovered knowledge, which was really thoughts. From that day on he had discovered thinking, he regarded the shining galaxies above his head as heaven and wanted with all his heart to go there, though the roads were rocky, rocky and the streets were narrow, narrow; he like Moses wanted to walk with God.

At first, he wanted to cross the Milky Way and dreamt that he might be taken up by rapture to walk in heaven's streets of gold like Elijah the prophet. He tried hard to reach the heavens, but his efforts were to no avail. As consolation he decided to remain here on earth and cross the river of dreams as a mammal. But occasionally, he would claim the light. His soul would soar to the heavens, breaking the glass ceiling of the skylight of heaven and soar beyond time and space. One day he wanted to cross the river of time. Although he could swim, he dared not chance it so late past the evening. He thought about this for a moment or so, and then called upon the crocodile brotherhood. Sobek their chief grew sympathetic to his tale and nominated one of their kind to take him across the river of blue ink. But first he had to promise Sobek his heart.

It was a moonlit, starry, starry night when he sat on the crocodile's back. Anancy marvelled at the image of the full moon that was reflected like a small yellow drum of cheese at the bottom of the river of blue ink. And he joked with the crocodile whether he would eat it later. The two engaged in chit chat: one example of the conversation between Anancy and his carrier went like this. Suddenly, the crocodile said:

"When can I have your heart?"

Anancy pretended not to hear.

"Will you give me your heart?"

"Yes", Anancy agreed, "but you agreed to take me across the river of time. I can't die on your back because you will fail if I drown."

"This is the river of blue ink", said the crocodile. "Do you agree to give me your heart?"

"Yes, a heart that is dry; not dripping with blood or wet with water. Sobek said a dry heart."

"I am not Sobek", the crocodile replied, "I am Curst, the King of Belgium."

"The deal is with Sobek, and he is your king."

"Crocodiles are reptiles. Reptiles do not have kings. Only apes have kings", said the crocodile.

"That's not quite right. Lions aren't apes and they have kings!"

The crocodile stopped halfway across the river of blue ink.

"Listen", he said, turning a sleepy eye, looking back at the monkey, "I am not here to argue with you, but from where all reptiles crawl, any being with a face like yours is an ape."

"Well, I never", the monkey intoned.

"I should turn back then." said the crocodile.

"Yes", said the monkey, "but then you will have failed to fetch me across the river of blue ink."

"How can I have this heart of yours, then? Is this a trick or a treat?" The crocodile muttered in exasperation.

"Take me across and if my feet are wet, my people will cut my heart out; hang it on a willow tree to dry, and you can have it later."

"Agreed", said the crocodile. "But when?"

"Under a satin sun and a satin moon. A satin full moon that is fully ripened and sphere shaped like a gala melon. Because I will give my heart, but my heart does not wish to die except under a southern sky."

"That's a paradox", the crocodile replied and laughed, chopping its jaws together and grinning his teeth. Its jaws chopping the water. "And we are in Cloud cuckoo land."

"It is a paradox of empire", the monkey replied, "The rivers of ink are estuaries of the heavenly river where souls drown."

Those were their last words.

Chapter Six

WELL READER, THE CHEEKY MONKEY never reached the shore. He was drowned and his body eaten by crocodiles. But his spirit resides in all living beings. The spirit of Anancy is in all things, be they man or beast. And all his dreams are in those persons who love goodness, and even in those who seem to hate goodness and beauty. As the crocodile said, life is a paradox. Others say that the great soul of Anancy became transmigrated into many diverse beings, one of whom is Ghede, whose metaphorical manifestation is the orisha Yemaya. And that is who I am when I am in my seventh house.

Dear reader you may well ask what am I physically? But nothing in my world is absolute, not even death, not even God. And I will tell you that I am neither man nor beast. But the spider God. Neither fully alive nor fully dead. I am his face disguised as a monkey, and a soul that thrives; that exists under a red satin sky with a golden satin sun, and a purple satin moon in the black book for the dead.

Believe me, I take as many forms as I will, and this is only one transformation. As I put this tale into being by now dear reader, you must realise that I am dead. I am the soul of Ghede (the abandoned sailor with a model ship on his head standing at the crossroads). He has fought many wars to free humanity. He has squandered his time fighting for everyone's causes, neglecting his own cry for liberation.

Again, I am Hanuman (the monkey avatar of the Vedas) Europe's monkey man. I am that I am (the crocodile bait of America, too). The scourge of heaven and hell and despised of the earth. Recognize me? Another voice from the watery grave that is the sea.

Looking back on my more recent lives, I remember major events dearly as if they happened only yesterday. But other events that are only part—remembered, mirror events in—between: part – memory, part—dream. Yet others are like blurred images of the past which sometimes seem as if they are happening in the present and what seems my current lives: events continue passing before me as I, suppose, like dry pages of a book that are burnt brittle by sunlight, golden, veined and dark as autumn leaves, or darkened and stained as the colour of fields of dry tobacco leaves or chaffs of wheat, rows of dry leaves, some tinged with gold; such memories unfold, and yet, it seems that I have dreamt them all in the past, may be in my other lives, or perhaps, a future life still to come. I am in my thoughts, circular as a wheel.

Yet, you ask, who am I as mortal flesh? In the universal sense, I am me and I am you. In the theory of particulars of the forms, I was named after Joseph my paternal grandfather, who was lynched in February nineteen fifty-eight at Notting Hill, just a few days before I was born. My middle name is Linden - my maternal grandfather's name, and as family names go, I am a Solomon; a Morris; a Cumberbatch and a Levy as well, and my star sign is Capricorn.

They say just like Jesus, and in my fluid state, I am not born of woman. I transubstantiate into the bread of experience, and I am as intoxicant as red wine.

As far as I see my physical self, I am a spirit in a dream - drama whose entrance on the stage of this plane began with dreams dazzling as the sun, setting over the sea, that gleams in a bay rimmed like a small lake, late of an evening when twilight is near. And that is where my soul travels when I am at my best. When I am alone!

There are days when I feel that I am exiled from a sunny day that warmed all the creatures of this earth - from a midday when the earth was at peace and calmness descended from the horizon to the sea, to warm the souls of all mankind - or rudely awakened from a night when the moon was full, waxing with energy and with light, to a place of foreboding, a land landlocked, like a mindset of no return or change, like the impenetrable mindset of a barbarian.

And what of my success? Although the entrance to this life has been perfect and I have inherited a gene pool lavished with exciting potential, the crucial event that ought to have taken place to catapult the expectations of so great a mind soul as mine onto the centre stage of life has never materialized, yet I am Joseph the dreamer, a fruitful branch of a tree descendant of mortals that loved good. I am I said, neither now, nor then, but a genie that passes through walls, whether material walls of brick, stone or concrete, or the metaphysical walls of time. And I am tracing my exit from heaven to hell when I lost the innocence of paradise. I am Los!

Before I died, we were moving, leaving the comfort of the neighbourhood where I had been brought up and there was a hollowness in my soul, my heart too, was heavy, and I felt alone, so I went for a walk.

Chapter Seven

I WAS WALKING UP THE HILL where the old church stood when I saw her, a girl about my age, thirteen (or so I thought at the time), and with the most perfect limbs and beautiful body that I had ever seen. This was in Camp Hill Church Cemetery, and I knew she was a strange spirit passing through the walls of time because I knew all the young girls in the area, and she too must have felt alone; her body language told me. Therefore, I felt something magnetic between us when we finally spoke, as we were at once alike and, in other ways, so unlike. But there was strong chemistry.

Siobhan was sixteen years old; copper gold, her olive skin shone; glowed like molten metal in the afternoon sun. And she had the clearest blue eyes I had ever seen; fine teeth and a smile that made me feel like a Hollywood hero meeting his leading lady starlet on the set of a movie for the first time. The chemistry was intense, and after we spoke, she decided to take me home to meet her mother.

Half an hour later we arrived in Halley Green, the green, leafy suburb that boasted the local college where it was my ambition to study after my CSE (Certificate of Secondary Education) examinations. We were still holding hands when she walked me up the short path to her front door. Her mother was standing in the passage as we entered and smiled a greeting; her face like her daughter's, but she was pale as marble but just as beautiful, and the child she held in her arms was also equally beautiful. My heart sank. I knew it was her child; it looked the living stamp of her.

"What have we ere?" the woman clucked. Holding the child on her right hip, "See, mommy is here," and she turned to me, "This is her boy, you know, ah!" The child looked like a street urchin that reminded me of pictures that I had seen of the supposed baby Jesus. "You look like Harry Belafonte". I smiled more out of fear than pleasure for I was anxious. It was a similar feeling that I often felt when mother scolded me.

It was sudden. There was a rush from the bladder to the urethra; there before this woman and the love of my life, I almost wet myself. It felt almost like those days when mother would take the strap to me: her taking it brought the desired effect of fear and loathing of losing her love, and guilt for having upset her, rather than the strokes of the strap, which were always ineffectual – almost comical, and with this fear of losing her love, often I would wet myself, and for days after that, full obedience would follow, for after all, I was her child; hers and my father's.

"Could I … could I use the bathroom, please?" I was embarrassed and ashamed, was that my voice, I thought. Yet, it was my voice after all.

"Go straight ahead to the back of the kitchen!"

So, I went and while relieving myself, my thoughts were racing. My parents might think the child was mine, that I had been hiding it; mother would kill me; father would do nothing to prevent it … father would kill me, mother would die … father would go to gaol. There would be consequences; gossips and rumours in the small, tight knit community of kith and kin; chants of disgrace, people would hear that I had a child, that I was a father so young … eleven, and hiding it from everyone for two years, two whole years; that I had been deceiving everyone, including my parents and, the Bible bashing entered my head:

> "Honour thy mother and thy father that thy days may be
> long in the land.…" the blue beat records sang this.

This passage from Ecclesiastes had been put to ska music. My heart was beating faster than I could run, my palms were sweating … I almost urinated on the floor. I was afraid! The song continued in my head:

> "Children obey your parents in the lord, for this is the law
> of the prophets.…"

Then came the chorus, part of which was the Golden Rule:

> "Do unto others, as they would do to you!"

Chapter Eight

T HAT DAY I FIRMLY BELIEVED that is exactly how Moses received the Ten Commandments from heaven: from a voice in the wilderness of his own head; rules planted there by a parent or, some adult seeking control over his life and infecting him to control the lives of others. I had told the Sunday school teacher this one Sunday at church, but she had just dismissed it as fancy talk by me. And I didn't argue with her because she was a woman of strength and strong, uncompromising faith. I had a chance to suggest this to the male Sunday school teacher who also was sceptical.

After that and he said that it sounded like a brilliant idea and had even called me brilliant. So, I wasn't afraid when voices came into my head, at least, not at that stage in my life. They were accepted just as I imagined Moses and all the prophets of time must have felt. Therefore, from an early age I developed my own understanding of ideas and how important they were to infect people and to make the world itself. I thought, then, that the world was built of ideas, and that adults were responsible for the confusion like the Tower of Babel and that they blamed God for their faults.

His name was used to cover up their mistakes and to carry on their battles, like wars, brawls, bullying, domestic violence, fighting and all manner of felonies; and that they spent most of their lives having sex; making babies; and killing themselves and others; sometimes even children as well, because that is what having power meant to human beings.

They blamed God for everything. God was everything and everything was God. Therefore, he was the one to blame, and when that did not work they blamed the devil, who obviously was an adult, and their good friend, and I could see that they admired him most, and even loved him more than they loved God because they were always saying that he made them do this, and he made them do that, and some adults would say to children, "You have the devil in you!" From where I am standing it is plain to see that with them, he was more popular than Jesus. Therefore, I was afraid of most adults as they seemed mostly violent and scary people, especially, the teachers at school and the famous ones who appeared on television. And in a way, I was a little afraid of this woman, because I had so many thoughts going round and round like a carousel in my head that made my mind confused. These thoughts racing through my mind, I considered that she might even be a witch or not human at all, but a demon, and that may be Siobhan was a spirit child.

I flushed, washed my hands, and returned drying my hands in my kerchief. Siobhan smiled; my discomfiture was obvious. The mother had that I told you so look on her face that showed resignation. So when I said I would be back to pick her up to take her to the Deritend Civic Hall later that evening to the disco, looking back now, she must have known that I could not handle a relationship that included a child, and I hoped that she would console Siobhan for me, because

I was only a child, and I was sad because she was a child herself, for in those days our parents ruled by fear, foreboding and respect, and looking back, I see now that perhaps, it was a good thing, because Siobhan was so beautiful that I wanted to marry her, but I had no money and could not even care for myself, so how could I have cared for a child?

I say this because like all young people of this world, I would wage an unconscious rebellion against the rule of my parents, and yet it would be their values that would shape my rebellion and eventually take over my life. Parents are powerful people; they have seen you at your most vulnerable and know you for what you are. Even when they are dead, you remain their child. I remember feeling a slight resentment against mother and father when I first realized the extent of their power over my life.

"So, what is your name?" the mother asked, fixing me with a stare.

"Joseph Solomon," I said, almost embarrassed, because I had so much pride in my name, and added, as if she ought to know "my people are mostly from Kingston." and she smiled, with a twinkle in her eyes.

This undying pride was all Aunt Bertha's training. She felt I had to know where I was from with no hesitation. Aunty Bertha, would say:

> "One day you should go to Kingston; go to the sweepstake,
>
> you will like the horse racing and to walk down Kings
>
> Street near the emporium. Yes, you will like Kingston
>
> Town."

She would remind me as I sat in her room, while she paged through the magazine about the people of the Ras Tafari that I had picked up at the airport. After that day, I overheard her and father talking in hushed tones and when I walked into the kitchen, they changed the subject and she remarked that the Rastas were taking a substance called ganja; and the magazine with black people with long hair that made their own shoes and music disappeared.

Chapter Nine

THIS WAS NINETEEN SIXTY - eight and I did not argue, I just accepted it, for Aunty Bertha was from Jamaica and knew best; knew all about the Rastafari and about Poko and quadrille and mento, and about Obeah and the black arts, and blue beat and the calypso too. And like her, my parents – the elders of my family, they all insisted that I should never eat from people, but what they meant was people they did not know.

So, when the mother offered me a drink, I politely refused on their account, but also because the place smelt too much of children. The smell of the child was so strong and the domestic scent so overpowering that I felt sick; felt like running away. It was like dish water perfume: smelling of soap and grease at the same time.

Siobhan wanted to hold my hand again, so I let her, and as she walked me to the door, I felt the urge to put my hand around her beautifully slim waist but stopped myself, as if instinctively, I knew that I had to let her go. So, we said goodbye at the gate where I gave the impression that I would be back. But I knew I would not. The baby would be a problem.

On the High Road, I stood nervously waiting for a bus, and pondered the meaning of our meeting and being taken home to her mother's house the very same day; how things had moved so fast and became impatient. But just as I was getting more agitated by the minute, the bus arrived. I jumped on, paid the bus conductor and it sped off in the direction of Brooklands.

Simultaneously, many images rushed through my mind. Siobhan was the most beautiful girl I had ever seen. But I was heartbroken about the baby. How would it be possible to gain my parent's permission to marry her with a child? It meant nothing that the child looked white. At thirteen I would have signed my own death warrant had I fathered a child. And Aunty Bertha would make me feel bad; she would make me feel so uncomfortable with her persuasive arguments; and all about obedience and sin. The others would join the crisis, singularly, I imagined them saying among themselves "Let me talk to him!"

There I would not be able or strong enough to cope with any of them; they would box me in and subject me to questions after questions after questions; not let me go out, and in the end, I would say where I had been. Then I would have bigger trouble, and perhaps, a beating or a threat of it from mother, while Aunty Bertha would intervene, just in time to stop it happening, just after I had confessed, but I would have trouble, which I did not like having in the house; not with mother, father or Aunty Bertha, and then Marilyn will come with her big sister—little—brother thing and try to act the adult with me.

Sometimes I had to give account where I went, what I had to eat if any, who I spoke to and who they or their parents were. I would imagine that I was a double agent, telling stories to two different enemies: the Jamaican secret police in the form of mother, father and Aunty Bertha: their chief interrogator, and the friends and acquaintances that I would meet from the different islands. Aunty Bertha one day said that I was telling different parts of the truth to different people, but all she really wanted was the core, like the inside of an apple where the seeds were, the real part that belonged to the house rules.

So, I realized that I had to be very careful when I answered their questions. This led me to believe that I was living a double life, I was taking part in a drama and sometimes I was a detective, while at other times a spy: a secret double agent, working for myself and giving each side the version of the truth that they wanted at that precise moment.

One day Aunty Bertha said that I should become a lawyer as I was very philosophical with versions of the truth. But despite all that, they always caught me out; somehow, I felt that I would not be able to handle them if they asked if I was no longer a virgin. This was very embarrassing for me, but they did not care, how I would get angry and frantic, they would just ask the question and smile or laugh, and Uncle Jeroboam would say, "Don't mind them, father did the same thing to Natty and Morris here; he did the same to them, but not to me. Because I didn't like dancing. They did but I only dance waltz." And they would laugh, which only added to my embarrassment, and mother would whisper to father afterwards, and Aunty Bertha would say, "Why you so shy if we ask a question?"

Every so often they would watch me dancing in the living room, or at a party and they would intrude in my private life, with sudden questions. Just like that, straight out of the blue, and sometimes in front of people. It did not really matter to them that people were there or that I felt embarrassed. They would look at me and lock their eyes with mine and smile and suddenly the question would pop out of their mouths. And I would freeze and become annoyed and angry and stop dancing and get frantic with my cousins if they teased and when they teased and teased and I could not take it anymore, I would just give them a lash and they would run and cry, even though they were my age or older than me.

Then I would get into trouble and mother and father would say "If you ever get any girl with child, we will kill you!" And invariably, mother would add "If you playin' the man, I and you at logger heads, because two man can't live in a house and man give dey woman money, and you have neither house, money nor car."

Mostly, I didn't know then that both boys and girls could be virgins, until Aunty Bertha told me that I should try to stay pure for as long as possible because sex was responsible for greater knowledge of someone else, and that it was spiritual like imparting knowledge to a child, and I decided then to wait before I had sex, because I did not want my head to spin like it did when I went on the roundabout in the park, or my eyes to roll, and certainly I did not want the fruit of the tree of knowledge because it was too much responsibility to pass on all that knowledge, or share it with anyone.

But the funny thing was that mother and father would sometimes say that Marilyn had better hurry up and give them a grandchild because they wanted one or two, three, or may be more. But with me they said I was too young and not yet ready to lose my innocence. They called it my virginity.

There were threats, that they would kill me and go to prison or hang for the crime because they would have diminished responsibilities. Which, at first sounded like music, like a diminished note "c" or "d", because I knew that father and mother loved music, until Aunty Bertha explained that it was a state of mind so emotional that people forgot what they were doing, but they did it anyway. I laughed and said, "Diminished responsibilities", and I wandered if soldiers had diminished responsibilities when they went to war. But Aunty Bertha said, I had to solve that knowledge for myself, so I remained confused about the word "diminished", like something getting lesser and lesser until there was none. Just like that, straight to nought; nothing left.

Mother and father had threatened me with death if I had a child before I were a man, several times, and, although Aunty Bertha had said, "Don't believe them," I always believed that they would kill and diminish me, which I felt they had the right to do; to take my life because they had given life to me. They had every right because they were my parents, and I was their child. It was the way they had taught me, and it was hard for people outside the family to understand but we had then for our parents a fear engendered love, and they worked from dawn to dusk to feed and clothe us. But if it was one thing I understood, it was that. You only became an adult at twenty-one, and a fully-fledged person within your own right then. So, turning the spectre over and over in my mind I decided halfway home to forget about the encounter with Siobhan, her mother, and the child.

Chapter Ten

W HEN I ARRIVED HOME, I sneaked passed Aunty Bertha's room; tip toed down the hallway and stole into my bedroom. I wanted to be unnoticed, so afraid that the look on my face would betray my guilt, I wanted to avoid their preying eyes, because they could get the truth where I had been out of me so easily. And if I gave one trouble, the other would pretend they had no idea what was going on, but then they would approach me with some strange remark, and gang up on me and bam, sooner or later I would give away my thoughts and feelings.

From since I had lived in that house with my family, I was aware that I was different to the other children in my street. There was my father Nathaniel, called Natty, and crazy about Slim Smith and his own singing; my mother Joycelyn, called Sweetie, who loved to cook and danced a lot with my father; my big sister Marilyn who was a bully, but pretty, and Aunty Bertha, the diplomat of the clan and it was her disinterested and matter of fact inquiries that always wore away my defences not to tell. Like when I was twelve years old and became ill and could not eat because the chicken in England tasted raw. I remember father and mother talking about my bowels and I was so embarrassed. Then Aunty Bertha intervened and asked me:

"You have any bowel movement yet?" I remember feeling a little embarrassed, what does my bowel movement have to do with these people? I thought. After all, I am an individual in my own right now and my bowel movement was entirely my own business, until I remembered that Aunty Bertha was a nurse, and mother and father knew I would see their asking such a question as babying me. When she said, "You must be constipated!" I said yes, and she smiled.

"See!" she said to mother and father, "You keep the child too shy," and all three laughed at my shyness. Mother gave me the Senna pods and I just took them, and, in an hour, I went. I felt good afterwards, because I was no longer bloated and restless, as if I could not concentrate on anything, especially my music playing in the living room. That was what among other things which made me different to the children in my street. I could use the living room, and to play their records. I had no idea where the records came from but every time there were new releases the forty fives just appeared in the radiogram, and I would stack and play them, fascinated at how each single fell and played one on top of the other. At christenings and parties, I would do the mash potato, the twist, the limbo, the ska, and the Poko dances and the adults would give me money. And Aunty Bertha was especially proud because I knew all about Jamaican and Trinidad music, because mother's grandfather came from Trinidad to Jamaica with the West Indian Regiment and became a calypso singer in Clarendon. I was a rude boy, and a saga boy, too.

Chapter Eleven

MARILYN WAS GETTING MARRIED, AND father did not know her fiancé because he came neither from Jamaica nor Trinidad and he was told that he was not into music: father could only relate to people by way of music and father's best friend Willie Doe, said that not only was Jimmy Mackintosh not into music but also, he was a "small island." Aunty Bertha was annoyed and kept pointing out that Guyana was the largest West Indian country, and not really an island, but Willie Doe said to her: "Well, it's a small island any way," and the next thing we knew Aunty Bertha had banned him from the wedding. She said in a strange dialect that I was fast becoming accustomed to hearing and understand again: "Damn feisty ignoramus man!" and everyone started laughing; then she spoke normal again, this time addressed to my father: "I don't want any peasant attitudes around me nephew. Children take in a lot of things, and we want to leave positive legacy."

At first, he argued but then Marilyn joined in and mother too, and he then agreed that his best friend should be banned since he insulted Jimmy Mackintosh at the domino table one night and there was a lot of noise in the back where they all came to play dominoes and listen to Iron Sound. Aunty Bertha said that Jimmy was a good person, he was tall and always made everybody laugh and did not really care who liked him or not, he just assumed that people had to because he was very tall and handsome, and always wore Guyanese gold, which was the best, and had a gold tooth and always looked groomed, and was fussy about food and clothes, just like Marilyn, and she added, a little crazy too, loving and nice to his friends but bad tempered and dangerous to his enemies, just like Jamaicans. When I heard that; you see when she said that I decided that it was a good thing that I was bombastic when I meet Jimmy Mackintosh, because I had to pay careful attention and use my best eye to observe him properly to see where he was coming from, so that I could make good tallawah.

Aunty Bertha was quick to update me, about the wedding, how it would be grand and there would be a lot of people there and dancing and music and plenty of nice young girls my age and she laughed, and that there would be something called the honeymoon, and other plans and that there were a lot of other bad people from the islands who would be there and that some of them were very bad people, really bad, and how I had to protect myself from them because I should always remember that I was born in a city that had inspired a song.

Suddenly, I was thirteen years old and leaving the house in Brooklands and Aunty Bertha was dying, and I was lonely and sad, so I went for a walk and met this red skin girl, and went back home to tip toe pass her room, and I wanted to cry, but I could not cry because my heart was breaking on two counts; because my heart was breaking in two, and I could not decide which one to cry for, and then we were moving to a place I had only heard about. There were so many things that were making me sad, so I decided not to cry for anything or anyone. But I could hear her stirring, so I knocked the door and went in to sit on the Ottoman, and when she felt my presence, she looked around and smiled.

Chapter Twelve

WE MOVED TO WATERSTON, A little village strung between Kingswinford and Wolverhampton. At fourteen years old, I was now taller than most boys my age, and no longer went to school, so I found little jobs working at the mill in Kingswinford. Mother gave up her job to look after Aunty Bertha and father continued his factory job in Willenhall, and to keep in touch with our friends in Handsworth he bought a new Jaguar, and life seemed more normal as the buses were unreliable and the people hostile, but the Solomon family is built on the backbones of tough survivors. Father would say his grandfather gave them a motto: "I trod this earth and fear only God; no man!" Sundays we went to church, and every Saturday we had a wedding or christening to go to, and even Aunty Bertha seemed not so ill with the new move and without the cares of looking after other people, she concentrated on getting well, and I even got a better job on the bins and refused to start college as I had fallen head over heels for money, because money carried the head of the Royal Mint. I got the taste for money from my mother's father's people the Cumberbatch, who came out of San Fernando, South Trinidad.

In a way, I was glad my parents were so well connected and seemed to have people from different islands dropping in even though we lived so far from Handsworth. Because they always gave me ten-shilling notes for my little bank, which I kept on the dresser in my room. I got a job early because I always had money in my little bank.

But because of my age I was encouraged by Pat McNally, the supervisor to apply for college. I applied to Cadburys in West Birmingham and only worked two days a week. On the second day at college, one of the senior teachers called me to his office, when I was learning history and explained why they had to let me go, because the deputy head of my old school had said that he could see no purpose for me to attend college as it would only give me big ideas about myself and my people and therefore it would be no use.

The senior said he was sorry, but I had taken a knife to school once, and I had to leave the class immediately, and not apply to the college anymore. I said I was sorry, but there was no mercy for me, no forgiveness of my past sins. He said, "Leave now; leave quietly and we won't call the police."

I left my books and went back to the bins where I was happy, and at times Pat McNally would tease me with the saying "No blacks; no dogs; no Irish". And I thought it funny and would laugh, until I cried. But I still loved myself and my people and all the oppressed peoples of the world.

Aunty Bertha said we shared a common humanity and I was consoled by her kind words and Pat's sense of humour, which was so true to what was really happening around me, and which was the reason I walked out of school one day and never went back, for the teachers would say that black people were stupid and I could not take that; then one day the same deputy who had become headmaster when the head master died, said that Paddy was a Mick, and Paddy took a chair to his head, and they expelled him, so I walked away from provocations and endured the battle, because that was the way things were in those days for us children going to school in England, the only teachers who weren't resentful were the ones that King Jaja referred to as the Welsh.

We would say he came from Swansea and his name is Mr Colonette, or his name is Hughes, or Travers and he comes from Llandudno, and he would say "Yeah man, that's in Wales". I remember Travers and Hughes; Hughes said to me one day, "You care about the treatment of your people, don't you?" And I said "Yessuh." And he said, "I will give you a book to write down your ideas about what interests you and I won't look at it unless you want me to."

He gave me this book and I wrote about our people and how they were hunted like kangaroos on Aborigine Sundays and how they loved the land of Australia so much; saw every inch of it as sacred, especially, down south in Queensland. I showed it to him one day and he said, "That's good; you have a vivid imagination." Then I wrote a poem because he said, "I bet you could write poetry." So, I started writing poetry and prose and everything. And King Jaja agreed that these people called the Welsh were a great people; people of the emotions, just like us; with an obsession for music, that showed humanity of a special nature. King Jaja was a good influence on us children, and everybody else as well, and he loved Aunty Bertha like rice loves peas, and chickens love corn.

One day I came home from the bins and found King Jaja, the very tower of a man bending over Aunty Bertha, and muttering what he called a verve, and mother said he was into the black arts, and had brought ginger roots that were grown atop soil and then buried in a hole to grow for three whole years. It smelt stronger than usual and made your lungs open out to the scent. After his verve he gave her tea from the holy thistle tree and took her for a drive in his Morris Minor, with the words "Barbados" on his side of the windscreen and "Jamaica" on the side where she sat. Aunty Bertha was laughing, and even Willie Doe who was visiting and who had sworn to be her own worst enemy was laughing with her and all the neighbours came out to see the show.

But most of the neighbours seemed resentful. We were only three families from the West Indies living in the new place, so when the rest of the family visited the people thought they had been invaded by wild Africans and kept pinning notes on the hedgerows that grew outside the gate that read "wild Africans go home." So, one day Uncle Jeroboam came from Handsworth with a couple of his friends and painted a large sign with flowers and palm trees on a long, broad piece of timber with the words "Kingston, Jamaica," and pinned it up at the front of the house. When I came from work Aunty Bertha was up and about and called me outside to see the sign, which I had passed unnoticed at the front of the house. "See!" she said, "I told you; we are Kingstonians."

There then was the living proof: for anything to be true for Aunty Bertha it either had to be verified in blue beat, kaiso or calypso music, or written down on paper, before she would commit it to memory, otherwise it was not true. This was the modern world of science that Marcus Garvey had told them would be coming, since she was a young girl in Kingston, and to substantiate what she meant she found my christening papers that she had confiscated from her brother, with threats of Obeah and the black arts, if he did not willingly hand them over, with the proof from Kingston Anglican cathedral. "Sweetie, Sweetie!" she called, "Come quick naw!" and she smoothed the ruffled sheet of paper over, "You remember this; keep it away from Archips; here it is, positive legacy!" And she turned towards me:

"One day you will unite the islands. You will be father of the nations, and while my body is in the grave, and my bones broken and melted down ina England, you will recapture my spirit; spirit is everything, you see. You see black people, we never die, if we pass - over under a satin sun, and a satin moon, the spirit must say farewell to the earth under a southern sky."

On what was to be a rare occasion I asked, "What do you mean Aunty? Pastor talks about the resurrection of the body and all that, is that what you mean?" She smiled. "Now you are learning fast. You see, our souls go back to Africa, at that very point of time we pass - over into the land, and we exhale a strong breath and on some river in Africa the spirit will find its final resting place, until the next thousand years, and then we come again, our people not born to die. But they must pass - over under a satin sun or a satin moon: that is the best way to die!"

It all seemed so much knowledge and wisdom, that I was afraid of growing up as it seemed to me then that with the increase of age comes more and more wisdom and that this was a big, big responsibility, and one which I had to pass on to my children. So, I decided then not to have any children of my own when I grew up, because I would have to teach them so much. I was hungry, but I sat with her outside the back and listened until the sun began to set as it was summer. When daylight dimmed, we looked for the satin moon, but it was never there.

In summertime we would light barbecues round the back and cook chicken and mackerel and even green bananas, but we kept to ourselves as the neighbours were afraid of our family ties with Handsworth, even though we tried to make friends, not many of them would reply when we greeted them morning or afternoon, or even good evening. But whenever we sat out the back, someone would come out and peep at us.

Marilyn and Jimmy Mackintosh turned up suddenly, with their car pumping out "Sally Brown" the strumming banjo was irresistible, and Aunty Bertha got up to dance, the neighbours who must have been disturbed by the noise at the front came around the back when Jimmy hitched up Iron Sound and turned up the volume maximum. Through the fence a teenager about my age peeked through the lattice and smiled directly at me. Aunty Bertha stopped dancing and said to me.

"There's your friend, give him a barbecue potato, you know they are delicious."

I smiled back, a little reluctantly, and forked a sweet potato from the fire wrapped it in a leaf and said: "Here ye are its vegetarian." He took it, though I thought more out of politeness than anything else; he did not even seem curious, but it was the music that attracted him.

"Is that rock 'n roll?" he asked. "No; its kaiso," I replied. "Kaiso music from Gemaica,"

"Where is that?" he asked. "Africa?"

"Yes" I replied. Aunty Bertha was there listening and had always taught me that we were Africans, so I didn't want to disappoint her.

Jimmy Mackintosh danced with Marilyn and Aunty Bertha encouraged them, and soon mother came out and her and Aunty Bertha were dancing, and my new friend Jay from next door looked surprised, because he had never heard a Sound System before, or music so loud. Because of that he asked his parents if he could come over and they must have said yes, because he walked round the front and came over and watched while I showed him the ska.

We had an enjoyable time until father came home and was cross because he said Jimmy Mackintosh had no right to hitch up Iron Sound without his permission. But Aunty Bertha started talking about Orange Street back in the days when they were youngsters and all the fun they used to have, and so he let Jimmy Mackintosh turn a few more tunes and we had a little jamboree.

Chapter Thirteen

AFTER THAT FATHER SEEMED TO like his son-in-law, and even forgot that he came from Guyana, so when he spoke about Jamaica, he just expected him to understand, and Jimmy Mackintosh would say yes, we have the same thing in Guyana, too, and Aunty Bertha would say: "See, we are all West Indies people." And Jimmy Mackintosh would look at me and say, "Crazy as hell." I really believed Jimmy Mackintosh felt that I was crazy because I had three islands blood in my veins and its true, and being conceited as hell, even then I still used to get frantic with people and even though quiet, I could still lose my temper bad, just like that. It was the rude boy era, and I suppose I just identified with Adolphus James, the hero of the song called "Rude Boy."

Although we had moved from Handsworth, everybody seemed to keep in touch because they were taking the partner hand money and buying cars or buying houses, because the banks wouldn't let us open accounts; they always referred us back to guarantors. We had to have two guarantors to have a bank account. So, the only way we could save money was to work for a big firm that liked you to save, or with the boxer or partner hand. The houses were needed because no one would rent us homes. Only the Pakistanis would help us out, and in those years, we stood shoulder to shoulder, although at times we did have our disagreements, but nothing serious. Then we all loved cars, because we needed to travel safely.

We called them armoured cars, you had to be careful when walking alone or at night. You had to be on the lookout; those days the teddy boys, and rockers would beat you up or even kill you if you were on foot; rode a bicycle or a motor bike, so cars were safer; safer even than buses. What made my new home so different was that we didn't have to move in fours anymore, at least, not in the outlying areas where there was the new breed of natives that called themselves Mods, and they dressed cool and liked our music, and they could dance as well.

Take my friend Jay from next door, the day I taught him ska he never looked back, and even came into Handsworth with us at parties, christenings and funerals. And then his sister Linda started looking over the fence and talking to me and listening to blue beat, especially when my cousins came from Handsworth to visit and when we kept parties, and before we knew it, bam, my cousin Rudy got her pregnant as they were both twenty one, and father stopped saying good morning and good evening to her parents, because he said he didn't want to encourage this mix – up, mix – up, business, because Rudy was already too red skinned, and with red hair and freckles he and Linda might have a dundus pickney, and then being dundus white the child will become confused.

But Aunty Bertha said that Uncle Dada, their mother's brother from Mandeville, being a Levy, was like that any way, and that father was talking like a dumdum. Aunty Bertha was thrilled and said that if the child was a girl, then she should have her middle name, which was Morris, but father objected saying he couldn't see why Papa Solomon had named his sister with a man's middle name any way, and was horrified because he said the child will have the same problems that Aunty Bertha had while she was growing up because people were astonished and confused by her middle name of Morris, which as far as he and his friends were concerned just didn't suit Aunty Bertha, because she was a girl, but she nonetheless, loved her name.

That same afternoon, Aunty Bertha who had been sitting at the dinner table, stood up suddenly, as she was taught in school, the way she must have been groomed to respond at call of the class register, or at social gatherings or Sunday School to affirm her name and identity and said: "Albertha Morris Levy Solomon, sir, that's me!" and as if she had forgotten the most important part of her identity, she added: "Yes, sir, from Kingston, sir! Jamaican born and bred". And she gave a salute.

Mother laughed until tears came to her eyes and ran down her face while father looked at his sister as if finally, he now had the proof that he had been waiting for, for so long to prove that his sister was unhinged, and smiled, nodded his head and went to prepare to visit his friend Willie Doe, I suspect to complain about Aunty Bertha's behaviour.

King Jaja, who was visiting at the time, supported her, and said, since father knew that she was head strong and the only sister, then it didn't matter what the name was, because a name is just a name, and father loved his sister any way, and they sometimes seemed too much alike and that's why they got into deep water and argued because both of them were two stubborn people, because he had been asking Aunty Bertha to marry him, but she kept using this cancer thing to scare him off with her stubbornness, so he sometimes couldn't come to terms with Jamaica people, anyway, because he thought they wouldn't be like Barbados people, but now he knew different, that like the other lot they were all bad people and damn well stubborn, feisty and rude to one another. And he sucked his teeth: "Una luv too much argument," he said.

Mother laughed, and father looked at King Jaja, as if he were a traitor to his kind, meaning men folk, and decided to leave early for the party to talk to somebody who would understand his point of view.

"Yes, go to your confidante – to confess – to your confessor, and let 'im nominate your sins," Aunty Berta said, as father searched for his car keys. "Damn feisty outa order man, telling me our papa give me the wrong name!" she scolded after him, while father hurried out of the house, slamming the front door.

When father left, King Jaja said to my mother, "Is this the way they are carrying on so?"

"I hear you is no better when you ready," mother said.

"Not me, you mean me brother and younger sister, and I always must cool them down," he said.

"So, I hear," mother said.

"It's only because Natty is hoping the child will be a boy, so he can have it called after his middle name", Aunty Bertha said.

Mother laughed. Aunty Bertha laughed even louder.

"Where is the joke?" asked King Jaja.

But the two women laughed even louder and kept a discrete silence. It was obvious that they were concealing something that was extremely hilarious to them but were too beside themselves to reply to his question. After they had calmed down, they both wiped their eyes.

"You tell him!", said mother.

"No, you tell", insisted Aunty Bertha, and she added, "You're his wife, Sweetie!"

"No, you do it", said mother.

Aunty Bertha wiped her eyes and blew her nose in a tissue; she looked at King Jaja earnestly and said: "My brother's full name is Nathaniel Archipas Dunbar Levy Solomon".

"Rass man, like you named after royalty", exclaimed King Jaja.

Both women laughed and looked at each other and Aunty Bertha ran to the bathroom laughing to wash her hands, both mother and King Jaja were laughing as well, then my aunt returned, and they continued with their work in the kitchen. "Let's wrap that one", said mother, pointing to the large rum and raisin cake. Aunty Bertha obeyed and looked at King Jaja.

"Well, he's got two odd ones there; what does Archippus got to do with Dunbar?" said King Jaja.

"That's too long a story to tell, right now", mother said.

"That's his name and nobody is prouder than him about his names. He wants his descendants to carry Archippus as a middle name", said Aunty Bertha.

"Yes, he can't wait for that one to come and for Marilyn to have pickney", said mother.

"I see!" said King Jaja. "He likes to have royal names".

"Yes, these names mean more to him than money", said Aunty Bertha.

"Yes", said King Jaja. And there was a pause, in which he seemed to ponder the real meaning of the names. "Well, what's in a name any way?" he shrugged.

Mother and Aunty Bertha laughed and agreed. "Not a lot", they said in unison.

Then after they had finished baking the rock cake, bulla and sweet bread, they wrapped them neatly in silver foil and tea towels and called me to carry them out to the car; we were going to Handsworth for yet another party. And mother and Aunty Bertha were still laughing when I joined them in King Jaja's car, with "Barbados" on the side where Aunty Bertha sat, and "Jamaica" on the other side where he sat, because he was teaching her to drive in the Morris Minor, but mother still pointed at the windscreen and laughed.

"You should put "King" and "Queen," on the windscreen of the next car you get," she said, and oddly enough King Jaja, said yes and went on to add that when Aunty Bertha marry him, he will put "King Jaja" on the driver's side and "Queen Bertha Morris Levy," on the other side of the windscreen so that people will know that we are serious people, and not a pappy show, because if they wanted a fight, we would fight if we had to, but that we didn't want to but didn't scare easily, and we only came here to help out the country, because they had come down and begged us to come here. That's why we came, because they needed some arduous work done, because they were tired and weary after the war.

Chapter Fourteen

T HEY WERE FIGHTING THE TEDDY boys at Snow Hill Station. They said all the islands had to defend our right to live in England. Suddenly there was a tide of bad feelings, like a hurricane let loose upon my world. Fighting got out of hand, the rude boys and the saga boys got crazier too, once sworn enemies, they gathered at Snow Hill with their knuckles bloodied, noses bloodied, kerchiefs once used to blow their noses in or wipe their faces tied over their heads like pirates, and I was especially proud of King Jaja, who brought Archippus home after he had bruised his knuckles badly. I watched two peaceful men who always made jokes turn into senseless machines that filled my childhood world with terror. Father came home to get his razor, and King Jaja must have driven as fast as he could to the house had to stop him from going back to Snow Hill, just outside Handsworth where the islands ganged together and sometimes fought each other to a standstill out of boredom.

That very day reminded me of the fight for independence, because Jamaica had left, and the federation broke up, and some among them were calling the others "small island", and they had retaliated. But they never used razors, knuckle dusters or cutlasses, just their fists. And when one man fell, they all backed off. After though, they had all come to terms with the breakup of the federation, and Lord Creator sang his "Independent Jamaica" and Mighty Sparrow sang "Jamaica have a rifle - chi Mind" adding "that is my opinion", and everybody laughed about it.

The fight with the British seems to have come from way back before any one of us, even my parents were born, and they sustained brutality, and were brutal themselves. When they were put down, the British did not back off like they did at first but piled on and kicked the fallen on the ground. When they saw this, they had learned a new way to fight. They called it more weight, and they taught us how to fight like that as well, so when we clashed at school, or coming from school, or at the ice rink, when one of us fell, we shouted man down, and when they fell, we shouted more weight, and Jamaica led the battle cry, and they all followed, with "more weight", "more weight".

The devil had clicked in father's mind, and he had rushed home to get his blades, but King Jaja said they had already proved their point and blocked the gate so father couldn't drive out. "You is a big man," he said. "You aint got time for this stupidness, besides we prove we point. Them can't stop us; not wan a dem can stop us; we is unstoppable. But we done prove we point".

"Lord mi gad have mercy on us. Have mercy sweet Jesas, have mercy on my poor people in their astonishment," bawled Aunty Bertha, ringing her hands. "Sweetie!" "Sweetie!" she called "Take control your husband!"

Mother was crying, "Stop him. Stop him; stop him lord." She cried, "Strike 'im dead, sweet Jesas!"

"You are asking the lord to take me?" father said, suddenly looking weary and bewildered; and he repeated as if in doubt.

"Sweetie, you ask the lord to take me?"

"Yes!" mother said if you are making violence to destroy me life and home," and she sucked her teeth, something I had never seen her do before, and added in disgust, "Mek 'im tek you, yes!"

That seemed to be the final cure that made father see sense, because mother was asking the saviour to take his life, and as he sat down in his astonishment, he looked hurt and pathetic, in a way that I had never seen him look before. Mother continued, clasping her hands, "Sweet Jesas," she said, "If it is possible, please take this bitter cup from my lips and forgive me lord, but if it is at all possible, please take my life or strike my husban' dead, dear lord, and saviour, sweet Jesas!"

After a while father calmed down, especially, when Uncle Jeroboam had driven from Handsworth to our house to report that Buckey had died since the attack. I watched my father cry and ring his hands and began muttering to himself. Uncle Jeroboam seemed to understand for he shook his head and sighed, then said "I know, we been tricked; we shoulda neva come a Inglan'."

Chapter Fifteen

I N THE MORNING AUNTY BERTHA did not come downstairs, so I didn't see her or hear her stir when I left for work and mother also was still not up when I left. But when I came home Uncle Jeroboam was still at the house and King Jaja came later with the bitters for Aunty Bertha and mother to drink because they had a great scare when father came home to get his razor, and it seemed as if he would get himself into deep, deep trouble, that could be really bad, because once you fall low you really sink fast and quickly as if you were lost in quicksand. I was going into the gate when Jay saw me and started asking about Rudy because Linda was anxious because they had heard that West Indians were like the Irish, he said, and she wanted news if he was all right.

"Rudy is not of that generation", I said to him. "He is more like us, English, and not given to bouts of political emotions," I assured him.

"Then who is that man that is staying at the house?" he asked.

"That's Rudy's father, I said, and added "I think he will want to talk to your parents soon, mebbe by Sunday, because he's been here for a few days now and I think he is spending a week."

The next day Aunty Bertha and mother were up and around the house again and it seemed that the medicine of ginger, bitters, wild garlic, and holy sickle that King Jaja bought had cured them. He had even bought a special drink for father, as Uncle Jeroboam had been staying over and liked the medicine that King Jaja distilled in his room in Wolverhampton, and had convinced father to have a bottle, but King Jaja bought father two bottles for the price of one, and a couple of new forty fives, which I had played in the living room.

But this music was different, it came from America and King Jaja liked it so much, and father played them and said it was like calypso, and blues and he called it rock 'n roll, and Jay next door loved it when he heard it. So, we had music from America that sounded almost like ours and it was fun, because as Aunty Bertha said,

"Black people just love to dance, even without music; you just click your second fingers and thumb or flick your wrist to hit your first finger onto your second finger and thumb and biff, you just catch a beat and move to it, just so," she said and started to dance, when the music stopped playing and everybody laughed while we were out the back and Iron Sound was hitched up to maximum.

But it was Marilyn and Jimmy Mackintosh that could do the dance good; that could dance to this latest music as good as they danced to our music, and Jimmy Mackintosh said that it was really the same, because it came out of Africa, and Aunty Bertha said, "See, I told you we are Africans."

This new music was so inspiring, and then we had more of it until Jamaica started making it too, and it came to us in big boxes, and more calypso came out of Trinidad too, and father went into the cellar one day and came out with what he called jazz, and some country and western and stopped going into Snow Hill to drink with his odd friends, but stayed at home and played Jim Reeves or Ray Charles or Fats Domino's music, but there was a change come over him, because mother bought a new bed and put it in Aunty Bertha's room, and he slept alone in the bedroom that they once shared together.

There was a change come over Aunty Bertha as well, because she didn't argue with father anymore. While once she would give the impression that she might marry King Jaja, she now discouraged it and put everything into going to church on Sundays. Both her and mother became Sunday school teachers and neither of them danced as much anymore but played another type of music that entered our house which they called gospel music, and they prayed a lot to sweet Jesas, whom they said was crucified and died for our sins. But I couldn't believe it, no matter how hard I tried because to me it just didn't make sense, because I couldn't see how people would know what God looked like since no one alive had ever seen him.

But then they were baptized with his blood one Sunday evening, and the people from church said that he was the lamb of God that had to be crucified for our sins, and I thought it was even crazier, because I couldn't see how a human being could become a lamb and God at the same time, and since no one could explain anything to me I started smoking ganja and refused to go to church. Then I was alone in the wilderness, and one day I started hearing voices and lost my sense of time and belonging. It was as if I had stumbled and fallen into the cave like where Joseph's brothers had imprisoned him.

About this time certain bearded men began to appear among us. They wore pretty colours of red, green, and gold, and sometimes combined with a sash of black. Our parents warned us against talking to such men when we met them on the streets. They said they were the black heart men that carried off children, and either murdered or returned them completely changed.

But this was England and we laughed at such things. They were easily avoided on the streets, but not at wedding receptions, shebeens and christenings. Like the dreadlocks men that I had seen in my magazine they had bloodshot eyes, were generally amicable, but could be fierce if you ever trod on their shoes, accidentally, or otherwise. We had the same fear of them as our parents had for the previous generation, and their beards really scared us. These were the first Rasta men in England, and they came from all the islands. They knew the magical trick how to stick rizla papers together and roll ganja. One Sunday, they gave me some.

This made me disappear for some days without saying where I was going and refusing to answer their questions at home, where I had been. In fact, I started visiting my black power friends and the hippy friends and staying over and going to parties, but both were so confusing that I would not see them for a long time, until I felt like it again. But I would buy ganja from the Rastas and smoke it round the back or go to the fields along the river with Jay and we would smoke it there, lying on our backs looking up at the clouds forming and the birds flying in the air. And sometimes I felt as if I was in paradise, because I liked smoking the herb. About this time a few Rastamen turned to quite a lot in that space of to me, before I left school. They claimed it was the healing of the nation. But our parents shunned them and called them crazy.

At first it started at the shebeens where I went with my school friends who were still at school; I had already left school and was working so I couldn't see if they could do it why I couldn't either. It started off one Sunday afternoon when we went from a family christening to a daytime Sunday blues in Winston Green, just down the road from Handsworth, and this girl called Precious was reading this book called "Lady Chatterley's Lover." She said she liked me.

I was fascinated by the language, and she showed me a couple of pages; I had heard of it before but never seen or read it and I was amazed; she was twenty and getting ready to give it away she said. She meant her virginity. So I said yes, while we were dancing, but after the dancing I changed my mind and she was angry with me, because she said she wanted me to, but then my friend Ravishing came over with a cigarette rolled with the ganja that he was smoking, blowing the smoke into the air like a big man, and he passed it to the girl then she passed it to me and after that I stood beside the big speaker box, with the sound thumping out and couldn't move. It felt like I was in paradise.

He held a corner, took her and rubbed and squeezed her down and she did the same to him and they danced and danced and left together. I had to make it back to Handsworth on my own, and I was so drunk that I got lost and ended up in Walsall and didn't get home until midnight. Father was waiting for me when I got in, he was fuming, but all that I could do was laugh, and he said if that was the way I was going to live that I should leave so I packed a few things and left to live with my hippy friends in Whitmore. He followed me trying to stop me, but I refused to go back to the house with him. That was the first time I left home and refused to go back until it was my birthday and Rudy came to get me from where I was living with my white liberal hippy friends, whom I thought really appreciated art, music, and tasty food, until they decided to monopolize my stereo and relations between us became strained.

At school I had made friends with Richard. He grew up in Handsworth and had moved to Whitmore as he hated large built-up areas; then there was Kant, his girlfriend Joanne and Rage, the guitar player, so I had made friends with them, and we had kept in touch. It was great living with them, because I was working and making money and wanted to get away from my voices. But then Rudy turned up with Jimmy Mackintosh after a few months; packed my things and drove me back to Waterston. I was relieved to leave as the voices were getting louder and louder in my ears, telling me to do things to people and to myself. When I arrived home, father was in the cellar sorting out his records, Aunty Bertha was waiting at the gate and mother was in tears round the back. There was one of those great meetings when I had to answer every question and got so tired that I had fallen asleep in the living room while they had ganged up on me as always and I vowed secretly that when I ran away again that I will not come back. But I was exhausted and just wanted to sleep. Then I woke up and found myself downstairs and crept upstairs to bed. I had never been so tired before and was happy to fall fast asleep.

Chapter Sixteen

S UDDENLY, I WAS FOURTEEN, AND everybody descended on our household; there was a great cook up by Aunty Bertha, mother, and Aunty Divine. The girl cousins that I got along with best, were Rachael, Raina, Charlotte, and Henrietta arrived first. Aunty Divine was Uncle Charles' wife; he was born in Mandeville, just like Aunty Marva, but had moved to Kingston when he was eight years old. He did most of his partying at Hanover Street when he was a rude boy, dancing ska, but his wife Aunty Divine came from St Elizabeth, and was what we call a real red skinned woman. Rachael was like her, and Henrietta too, but Raina and Charlotte were not as light skinned. But just as pretty.

In fact, I liked Charlotte's complexion best; she was real shiny ebony, every part of her was like that. I used to see her body when we were younger and remember the tone of her skin, but at twelve we stopped not caring about her being a girl and me being a boy, and would hide our bodies from each other, or say sorry and look the other way, but I really loved all my cousins, but Charlotte was a dream, because she didn't know how pretty she was and liked the same things as me.

I ran downstairs all excited when they came and each of them gave me a kiss and Aunty Bertha said, "See, you have a family and we love you; we all love each other, and we love you as well." And I felt ashamed running off to live with strangers, even if it was only a few months, and they were good people. Then Rashida, Esme, Mimi and Ismay came later. But I was extremely excited for the boys to arrive and kept going out to the gate to see if their parents' cars had arrived. Then Jimmy Mackintosh turned up with Marilyn who drew me aside and started lashing me and crying, and no matter how Jimmy Mackintosh tried to get me away from her she would not let me go, she just lashed me on my back and said how I tried to kill her mother and father and Jimmy said to her; "Well, it's his parents too, so stop it now". But she let me go only to grab me again and Aunty Bertha called father to come and discipline his children. When father came Jimmy Mackintosh grabbed Marilyn and took her away from me, but she was still crying, and father took me upstairs to have a talk. I was really feeling bad because despite her bullying I knew my sister loved me like bun and cheese.

It was while I was upstairs with father that Abdi, Ishish, Laban, Jojo, Sallee and Lance arrived. It was then that Uncle Jeroboam finally had the courage to visit Jay's mother and father and they came over, because he had taken them some proper rum from Appleton's Estate.

Jay was at the bottom of the stairs, calling me and his father Eddie shouted. "Where is the birthday man, bring him on!" And when I came down stairs he had a pretty mouth organ in the key of "C" that he gave me and I thanked him for it and father welcomed him and his family into our home and himself poured him a drink of rum, and gave him lime water as a chaser, and mother spoke to his wife Carol and Uncle Jeroboam kissed Linda on the cheek and said she was beautiful and all the big people got together in one room and the young ones in a different room and people kept coming and others leaving and the music was maximum, and Uncle Jeroboam didn't have that talk with Linda and Jay's parents because Rudy came and stayed and then took her for a drive, and suddenly it was Sunday morning and the party was done.

We opened my presents, and I was very happy suddenly, and we were tired. So, everybody went to sleep, and that was when I heard that song for the first time: "Limbo". And it was beautiful. I heard the two versions one from Jamaica and the one from Trinidad, with Iron Sound turned up maximum; then "Brother David" played and Aunty Bertha came upstairs as if in a great big hurry like she was on a big mission and said to me "Did you hear the mento first, then the calypso and this ya wan a playre now; that is Poko; you can hear the beat: putuputumpum, putuputumpum, putuputumpum, putuputumpum!"

And I imagined Aunty Bertha with her head tied with a white scarf among the sweeping green hills of the Caribbean, dancing on the red earth of Jamaica to that same beat, to show that we are alive, that we are here to dance on the bones of the dead, where the soil is red as their blood, where the hibiscus grow among the black rocks, black as the skin of our people in islands sweeping in an arch from Trinidad, off the coast of Venezuela up to the Bahamas Islands, and taking in Cuba, because we are one people united by dungeon ships that a long time ago crossed the sea to bring us there, and I fell asleep listening to her voice, telling me tales of her Maroon great grandfather and all that Anancy history that sometimes hurt my head, so I was happy to doze off into a deep, deep sleep.

When I woke up at three o'clock in the afternoon that same song was still playing; but this was round the back. I heard the music drifting up from the window at the back up to my room, because Jimmy Mackintosh and Rudy were out the back and had hitched up Iron Sound again, and I could hear people talking and laughing. These were the best times, when after every birthday celebration everybody slept over and we woke to this big lunch because everybody had missed breakfast, so we just had one big feast that seemed to last throughout all day until the evening came and everybody went to their homes to prepare for school or work the next day. Feeling good, I stretched full out on my bed and flexed all my muscles. I had growing pains and knew that I was getting taller, so I was happy about my body, and my height was just above average for my age: I was five feet ten inches, and still growing. When I got out of bed and walked to the window Linda and Rudy were dancing; she seemed happy as Rudy showed her how to dance. Jimmy Mackintosh and Marilyn were shouting encouragement.

"C'mon girl," I heard Marilyn's voice above the music.

"Yeah; that's the way to dance it, Linda. Yeah, reach forward and turn!" I could hear Jimmy Mackintosh' voice exhorting her as well. They sounded to be having a wonderful time and were enjoying each other's company, when I heard Uncle Jeroboam calling Rudy to come inside for a moment or two, and to bring Linda; Linda was by now ready to have their baby and I was excited to have another cousin, especially, one living just next door.

The back door creaked, and I heard Rudy's voice inside the house, so I crept a third of the way down the stairs to listen. Then the front door opened, and Jay ran inside when mother opened the door to his parents. "Good evening, Mrs Solomon", he said and bounded up the stairs. Mother muttered a reply and welcomed his parents. They all moved into the living room and closed the door. Aunty Bertha was the first voice that I heard, and I knew she wouldn't talk too loudly so I put my finger to my lips to tell Jay to be silent and tip toed down the stairs. Whereas her voice was muttering at first, I could hear her clearly.

"This is not the way to do things my nephew; what example are you setting for the younger ones? What if Rachael or Raina, or any of the other girls were caught out like this, what would you expect the young man to do?"

"Why married them of course; that is the right thing to do. First comes love; then comes marriage; then comes a girl with her baby carriage." It was mother's voice.

"Horse and carriage" Aunty Bertha affirmed.

"Horse before the carriage not the carriage before the horse." Mother replied.

The others were silent; the talkative two seemed to be having a two-way conversation and, seemingly, had already made up their minds what the outcome would be. Rudy spoke, but all I could hear was the tenure of his voice; it seemed to be trembling as his two aunts were determined to marry him off to Linda, the epitome of the girl next door. Her parents could be heard in their attempts to put across their ideas, but Aunty Bertha and mother continued with their sayings: "First comes love … and after that marriage; and you love her, don't it?" That was Aunty Bertha's voice.

There was no clear answer from Rudy; so, mother reinforced it.

"The marriage bed is pleasing to the lord; it is better to marry than to burn."

"Ehem; ehem!" said Aunty Bertha. "Amen."

I could see that they had learned these sayings whilst still young and that they had been learned by constantly repeating so that like songs they had become part of their memory; hence their conversations were conducted in colourful sayings or part texts from the Bible when values were being upheld in practical ways. They must have learnt such sayings at Sunday School, I thought.

"Green are the leaves among the vines," recited mother.

"I took you for a friend of mine; I chose you from among the rest," repeated Aunty Bertha.

"Cause you are the one I love the best," mother replied.

Uncle Jeroboam interjected. "Listen I tired this damn talk. Look Rudy what is your intention with this young lady?"

"Honourable!" Rudy replied.

Suddenly, Aunty Bertha and mother were willing to listen, I gathered that as they became quiet.

"Good!" said Uncle jeroboam.

"Hon –our – able; good, that's a good start.

"You don't have to marry her if you don't want to, you know."

That was Eddie's voice; and a brave thing to say I thought, with mother and Aunty Bertha already reading the morality act about marriage being sacred and holy.

"Don't encourage it," said mother, "They have to do the right thing, marriage is completely in the question."

"Yes; completely into the question", Aunty Bertha reinforced. "Yes, yes, of course!"

"There can be no doubt about it!" said mother.

Then I heard father's voice for the first time: "Right then, the young man said his intention is honourable; can't anybody hear properly in this family; he is willing to bite the bullet and settle down to married life, as best as he could. And believe me, he could not have made better choice, than Linda and here they have my blessing. Cheers!"

And I imagined them raising their glasses filled with Mountain Dew and toasting the intended bride and groom. Then they turned up the music and were talking, but what they said next was drowned out by the blue spot radiogram, turned up full to maximum.

But I thought about them in the living room and what really surprised me was father's turn around about not encouraging mix—up, mix—up business, and the way he had greeted them at the door, as if they were long lost relatives. Aunty Bertha had told him he had been acting like a dumdum, damn fool, and they had quarrelled and then made up. So, I supposed the adult world was filled with people who were forever changing their minds.

Jay was surprised that my family wanted Linda to marry Rudy, because he had told me that his daddy went on at her about having mixed up children, who eventually will have mixed up minds, but that his mother had called him a fool. So, we stood eavesdropping on them, and were amazed by the way they seemed to come to agreement so quickly. When Jay asked why Aunty Bertha and mother were so much for marriage, I told him that Queen Victoria was their godmother and the people of the West Indies loved what she stood for and really enjoyed having lots of children, but the more "stush" always supported her ideas on marriage. Besides, they loved dancing and making music and a wedding was always a good excuse to have a jump up. He said he could see that, because they even had dancing at funerals when he had come to Handsworth with us.

Just then Jimmy Mackintosh and Marilyn came in from round the back and I had to pretend that Jay and I had just come downstairs to drink some water. We rushed into the kitchen. But she looked at me and cut her eye, and stropped her teeth and said, "I watching you, you know," and she turned to Jay "Don't follow him, you know. Naw don't follow him!" But Jimmy Mackintosh put his arm around her waist and told her to calm down. Then he called her his sweet Demerara sugar darling and she let him touch her and she smiled.

But she didn't see that Jay looked at me and winked because he was two years older than me and already knew where the man put it when adults had sex; he had told me all about it when Linda first became pregnant. He said he had heard his mother Carol discussing it with Linda when she said she hadn't seen her monthly. And I thought that it must be like getting paid for when you work, because I got paid by the month then. But he said it was like bleeding every month to make way for children to come down from heaven, into the womb, which he said was like a house of eternity. But I suppose I was in the wilderness then, only just turned fourteen and understood how to do it, but had no idea of the other stages that made women bleed, so I felt sorry for them, because they had this thing every month, on account of their having close connections to heaven, where children came from after the man had put himself between their legs and they danced together for a long time, and they groaned and made noises like the tabbies did round the back at springtime.

Then after all that, suddenly, Aunty Bertha had given me a book called the "Lovers", and mother had bought a cyclopaedia that told you all about the human body, and then I understood everything. I kept wanting to do it at times, but other times I felt it was an entirely senseless act, and quite stupid. For then I would become embarrassed by my thoughts, and guilt would set in because mother and Aunty Bertha said that you had to be married to someone to do it with them, and I thought that's a lot of responsibility when you had to account to and care for somebody else, all because you did that with them. But on the other hand, I couldn't wait to grow up to do that because sometimes when I danced it felt good and a strange, but nice feeling happened to my body and also when I looked at my cousin Charlotte sometimes and she smiled I felt strange, but nice too, but I knew I couldn't marry her because she was my first cousin, and besides I loved her in a special way that Aunty Bertha called spiritual, which was more important than the other kind of love, and I didn't want to lose that kind of love for her, because one smile from her and she meant everything to me.

Chapter Seventeen

F ROM THAT DAY, PEOPLE CAME with all manner of presents to the house as they prepared for the wedding of the year. Aunty Bertha and mother had set the main cake with rum and raisins and kept baking samples to taste to see if the ingredients were mixed right. But when the ingredients were right, they both agreed that now that they were right, they had to get them perfectly right. Then when they were perfectly right, they said they had to get them perfectly right. That was when King Jaja's younger sister turned up with Blades, her Barbuda husband, who was the tallest man I had ever seen, even taller than Uncle Jeroboam and King Jaja himself. And they were tall men, just like father and Rudy, but Blades was the tallest of the tall, as Aunty Bertha said. But he went off with father somewhere in Willenhall to look for his brother Jim, who had married a Saxon girl, that's what he had called his sister - in - law as he described her "a nice looking Saxon girl by the name of Janet" he had said, letting the words roll off his tongue, and stressing the word "Saxon" as if he was tasting sugar; samples of cake, or coconut drops.

Blades had a way with stresses and intonations and spoke like a singer. Aunty Bertha said he had "talks". His wife thought so too, because she kept looking up at him as if hypnotized by his every word

"

and mesmerized by his face, which she couldn't see at eye level and kept tip—toeing every time she looked at him. She wasn't short, but it seemed to me that everyone under six feet looked much shorter when they had to look up at Blades. His wife's name was Blossom, whom I called taunty Blossom, and they had a daughter called Cherry, who was my match, so I called her Cherry Blossom, because she had that red, blue complexion that I loved so much on women.

So, I immediately felt funny, but nice with a strange feeling. My throat became flooded with saliva, my mouth dry and my heart began to pump blood faster and faster until I felt dizzy, and the voices in my head said: "Sweet Cherry Blossom; sweet, sweet, sweet!" Then while Blossom, Aunty Bertha and mother were disputing about the ingredients of the cake I called her round the back and when she came and smiled, she said, "I know you want to ravish me; I heard everything about you from Cousin Charlotte." And suddenly I was angry with Charlotte, I thought, why is it every time I had this strange feeling she had to be involved? "That Charlotte," I said, "I'll fix her, just watch."

"You can't", she replied "she is in love with Boy, and he is in love with her as well." And she looked me up and down, cutting her eye, "And she's your blood cousin; so, you can't."

"I don't mean it that way Cherry Blossom," I retorted, but still trying to hide my surprise.

"Cousin Charlotte will get a beating if Uncle Charlie knows about this boy friend called Boy," I said.

"No, he won't," she replied, laughing at the pun.

"How do you know that?" I asked. This time my heart was beating twice as fast. I felt jealous, as if my world had fallen apart. This was my favourite girl on the entire planet and the very thought of someone getting close to her was worrying. I never wanted her to marry anyone; not even to have a child for anyone and, besides, I hated the word Boy for a name. I plucked up the courage to ask "Who is this boy named Boy, anyway?"

She found my question humorous and laughed for a while. Then she said: "I don't know," dismissively, "I only heard about it from Henrietta."

"You see that, Henrietta, I'll fix her you see."

Cherry Blossom strupped her teeth, "You can fix anybody? You can't even even fix youself." I made to lash her one as I always did with my cousins but she ran back indoors and when I followed her Aunty Bertha came to the back to take the air, so I walked away and went to call for Jay over the garden fence. He did not answer, so I went to the front of the house where he let me in and stayed there for the rest of the evening, but thinking about Cherry Blossom and Charlotte's boyfriend and Henrietta, and everything, until I started hearing voices that I got so tired that I fell asleep listening to music in Jay's room after we had a cigarette stuffed with ganja. After all that I forgot about everything and went over and fell asleep so quickly, that I thought I would never wake up.

When I woke up the next morning I went to work, as usual, but came back at about three o'clock in the afternoon. This was on account that I couldn't go to the pub and sit inside with the other bin men; I always had to sit outside while they brought out my drink and I was getting fed up with this law about drinking for minors. But Pat would never allow me to join them in the pub. That afternoon I got so fed up and left for home without the customary drink at the pub with them. On arriving home, I bounded up the stairs into my room, and Cherry Blossom was fast asleep in my bed. She looked like a baby, and immediately, I could imagine her as a child going through all the various stages in my mind. I walked out of the room and went to the bathroom, where I freshened up, and joined everybody in the kitchen.

"This is the secret," Blossom said. "This is top secret; the ingredient is top secret. But the labour is free."

"That's," said Aunty Bertha.

"Be careful with this one," said mother. "She is a businesswoman and might want to make money off us; see! She has a twinkle in her eye," and she laughed.

"OK,OK, it's OK," said Aunty Bertha, playfully, winking at mother.

"Of course, it's OK; it got to be we chargin' you the same price as what you charge, we for the wedding; nothing more; nothing less," said taunty Blossom.

"OK, OK, tell Winnie to take it out a de partner hand", said mother.

"Agreed", said Aunty Bertha.

"Good!" said taunty Blossom. She was tasting the sample once more and invited mother and Aunty Bertha to taste. They followed suit and gave sighs of approval, then looked at each other, then at taunty Blossom and smiled.

"That is the flavour we want," said mother.

"Oh yes", said Aunty Bertha. "Good, thank you sister Blossom".

Taunty Blossom gave a sigh of relief. "Thank you; I glad you agree that is the right taste we been striving for and now we found it; now we can bake the cake, and everybody can have their prime slice at the wedding of the year."

"Glory be to the Almighty," Aunty Bertha and mother exclaimed. And they kissed taunty Blossom, one on either cheek.

There was the shuffling of feet. Cherry Blossom came bounding down the stairs and into the kitchen. I looked at her scoldingly, just in case she had felt my presence when I had entered the room when I first arrived from work, but she still looked dreamy and tired, and did not notice the scowl on my face, or if she had, chose to ignore it. In a sense, it's as if she was letting me know that although we were born the same day that there was a world of difference between us; that she was somehow more mature. This of course, I couldn't accept, because of her being a girl. But I liked her a lot and started feeling that strange thing in my body again, so I just tried to ignore it. But her I could not ignore, and it's as if she knew it; as if everybody in the kitchen knew it, and Aunty Bertha pretended that nothing was happening; nothing at all. But mother was in one of her moods again and said to taunty Blossom: "You don't have nobody asking about this one yet? Look how she whisked them eggs and then the flour to help us bake these cakes. Your child is a wonder."

Aunty Bertha who never could resist a remark by her sister – law replied "Yes, a wonderful girl; really wonderful."

"Thank you taunty and gaddy," she said and sat down around the table.

I was still standing and glad not to be too near her. She had that girlish smell about her as she spent most of her time showering and reading books in the bath than normal, and Aunty Bertha who tended to compete with mother for her affection was always buying her perfumes. In fact, Aunty Bertha was always buying all the girls' perfumes and asking private questions about how they washed themselves. They never seemed to be embarrassed like I was when she asked me such private questions, but took it naturally, and I think that was so because they were always getting pretty soaps and hints from her and mother about douching. It was through this that I learned that going to the toilet was not as simple as most human beings would have it, it was a big job and you had to wash your hands before and after and that the genitals, as Aunty Bertha had called it, and mother had laughed because she knew I would be embarrassed, had to be given a special bath as if it was a different body on your body.

Cherry Blossom smelled too sweet, and I was about to leave when mother said, "Sit and sample the cake and talk to your god - sister; you always running away when family come here, over to the Morrison's, like you don't like us". I sat down without a thought about sitting down, but my head filled over with other thoughts: Cherry Blossom was mother's god – child; no wonder she was asleep in my bed and was so arrogant with it. These girls, they get the best in this family.

Taunty Blossom looked at me and smiled, "Come and give you taunty a kiss," she said. I obeyed and moved forward as she turned one cheek then the other for me to kiss her. Cherry Blossom turned her face away and looked outside as I obeyed her mother. Aunty Bertha smiled and said, "Young people should always respect us; we are their elders; without this they stand the risk to die young. The lord said he will strike down the young and foolish."

"He is respectful, but too shy for a boy," mother said.

"I don't think so at all; he is a little bit bashful, but quite self-assured; women who can keep they tail part quiet will love him; not those who are doctored. Leave him alone; he aint want to have no woman wid fire under them," said taunty Blossom.

"Hot!" replied mother.

"Definitely not that type: a decent girl …winsome," Aunty Bertha said.

"No guinea hen, nor guinea fowl; no senseh fowl" said taunty Blossom.

"Xactly; a pretty girl. Someone like… someone like Cherry," mother said and laughed.

"Is that a proposal?" asked taunty Blossom?" her face animated.

"Could be," mother replied.

Aunty Bertha looked at me, solemnly, "Joseph you love Cherry, don't it? I could tell by the way you ignore her, and she is ignoring you too; we not stupid you know we can tell from the way onu ignoring' each other."

"Don't embarrass the young people them," said taunty Blossom. And don't even bother ask she nothin', she won't answer; that pretending little girl; if she thinks she will surprise us with a boyfriend in a rush, we will sort her out; she should get engaged then married. What do you think godmother?"

Mother laughed: "First comes love, then comes the engagement, then comes marriage and then grand pickney - them supposed to come after."

"Well godmother," taunty Blossom replied, and she looked at her daughter's face, "You hear that girl? I couldn't agree more!"

But Cherry Blossom lowered her eyes and stared past the other women blankly, as if she was seeing into the future. "OK then; I will marry him if he goes to university and becomes a doctor, or make something of himself, otherwise no! I don't like England; it's no place to live," and she smiled, a little embarrassed.

"Ehem! Listen to that said taunty Blossom. "Well, look pon that," and she stared at her daughter.

"Sounds like an ultimatum," Aunty Bertha said.

"And it's a good one!" said mother. "Excellent!"

"Well, he has his work cut out, and such a pretty, young wife to be at that," said Aunty Bertha.

But while all this was going on, I felt really uncomfortable and embarrassed and shy, and I was thinking if I had children with that girl, would I have to help her change nappies and feed the babies and give them a bath? and another thing, would I have to do what they call make love with her, and become close as one flesh and all of that nonsense that adults do? The thing is, she seemed to have accepted the adult world as a matter of fact, but I still had to come to terms with it. So, I was confused, but it was true that I had feelings for her that was like no other feelings I had ever felt before; not like I felt about Charlotte.

I was beginning to become more desperate when the front door opened, and father and Blades walked into the kitchen. The women quickly changed the subject. Boy I was so glad when they came in, so I ran outside to call for Jay at the back. Cherry Blossom's eyes followed me as I left. She had that wait and see look on her face and I suddenly felt scared of her, but still, I just went out the back as if I didn't really care.

Chapter Eighteen

I T WAS THE SECOND GREAT wedding of the year, and I was barely over the first, which was unexpected. When cousin Charlotte told Uncle Charlie that she wanted to become a nurse he refused to let her go for training, that is, until Aunty Bertha intervened, and Uncle Jeroboam told his youngest brother that he was unusual; not normal, and sucked his teeth at him about six times, all in one sentence. Then Charlotte could go for training, and they beat her and said that she could not see Boy anymore, because she had to be a virgin for her husband to be, who was coming up from Jamaica the next month. So, it was a quick fix wedding, because Boy they said was no name for any parents with common sense to call their child.

"Look me crosses," Aunty Bertha said. "What if they have a child and they call it Girl? The child's name would be Girl Boy. People would laugh at us. I don't know any West Indies people with any common sense who would name their pickney Boy," she added and strupped her teeth.

But mother corrected her: "Naw, the boy first name is Boy; and the child's name would be Girl, daughter of Boy, or Boy's daughter," she smiled and laughed, and Aunty Bertha laughed too. So that was it, they needed all the excuses they could to dissuade Charlotte and soon she was weaned off Boy.

So when Geremel, came up, on account of him being related to Uncle Charlie's wife some generations back, they all decided that it was a good match and cousin Charlotte was taken from the nurse's home where she was staying, because she was nursing at Dudley Road Hospital and living in, and although I liked Geremel, on account of him being uncle Dada's god son, I was still jealous of this marriage, because he would have my favourite girl cousin all to himself, and they would become one flesh. And soon they would be doing it like adults are supposed to do to show their love and affection for the ones they were in a sexual relationship with, which was different to the other kind of love that Aunty Bertha said was the other side of life, but that both came from God: sex—love and the other, love—love. Of course, I understood that my cousin was precious to me and to all of us because of the last one, but Geremel would have a little bit of love – love for her too, but more of sex – love, but we were underneath every surface, one family as Geremel was one of us any way, but far enough to have sex with Charlotte. I understood that was all right, but still I was jealous.

We descended on the Tower Ballroom at Edgbaston Reservoir, which was a large building that stood back from the rim of the water that circled the shore like a lake; there was a resident band that played the music called jazz, there were caterers who cooked the food and waiters and waitresses who replenished the tables with our type of food, and Charlotte was dressed in white because she had saved herself from Boy, for her husband who was the family's choice. Then after a while the band left, and they harnessed up Iron Sound and everybody cheered and started calling out "Natty! Natty! Natty!" and the MC introduced father and cracked a few jokes and started blowing air into the microphone and singing part of a calypso called "Jean and Dinah," and everybody laughed; joined in, and clapped. Father tested the sound: "123; 1- 23;1-2-3; 1234, testing, testing, testing. We always testing!" The crowd erupted in laughter, with whistles, hoots, and shouts and, the applause sounded like the syncopation of rain drops falling, the watery percussion coming from afar off, and reaching the ears as if a great wave had rose in the ocean; hurried ashore to wash over your entire body, and the feeling was good.

When this had died down, the MC sang: "the Yankees gone West Indians take over now"; and the people clapped and laughed and the mento music began with that hypnotic beat that everybody said Jamaica had captured from Trinidad, but which Aunty Berta said came from Africa. That it grabbed your bones and possessed your muscles as well as your soul, and to stop yourself from shaking, you just had to dance.

Then at midnight we all came out on to the shore of the reservoir. They set firecrackers up. And I heard great big clusters of crackling sounds, and when I looked up the sky was satin, and the moon was silk. And the bride threw her bridal bouquet behind her back. The happy couple left for their honeymoon in Italy, and we all cheered them off; then went home, happy as well, and immediately the next day they began preparations for another wedding. When I was young every Saturday was a wedding, and anyone could come.

The second great wedding of the year was not much different: after the church ceremony we all returned to The Tower Ballroom at Edgbaston Reservoir; it was as if the same caterers, waiters and waitresses were there, that the same band was there and the Morrisons seemed surprised among this great throng of black family that had turned out, dressed in the most dashing of clothes because everybody knew that that we West Indies people were the first to use brands that started in Trinidad; you can hear it in the calypso: "I want a sack, wid a pretty bow in mi back." I had a sack as a small boy in Jamaica – and a navy uniform the colour blue, of course, with a navy hat with string tied under my chin, and then the men would wear trilby hats, coats, and big leg trousers, and then the youngsters in drainpipe, from saga boys to rude boys. Trinidad and then Jamaica. Yes, I remember all that like as if it was just yesterday. And every time we saw a picture of our people in America it was the same style, like it was universal for us as if – as Aunty Bertha said it was in the genes.

True to his name and rude boy status, Rudy opened the floor with Linda and all the young people joined in and the older ones showed them how to dance the fancy stuff for the rock 'n roll, and the jazz and the calypso, and then came the ska. You see when the ska came out and Iron Sound was turned up high, the big speaker boxes vibrated like over size drums, because Jamaica had invented Sound System, and the whole party went Ska crazy, and when three ska music played one after the other everybody clapped the MC, and he came to the front of the stage; pretended to fall over the tip, and bowed three times and played them again, and somebody shouted "Tune!" three or four times; then everybody seemed to sway to the music, and drink and food flowed and then Rudy and Linda went to Leeds for their honeymoon and we went home late and slept until late Sunday evening. Then it was Monday morning, and we all went to work.

For my part, I was just beginning to like Cherry Blossom, but even though I had danced with her at both weddings I was still a little afraid of her, because she was like a little woman; the way she held me was so possessively that everybody laughed and said she would control me, so when Pat McNally got a place for me at university in Sheffield I just packed in September and only said goodbye to Aunty Bertha, my father and mother and the Morrisons who had become a permanent fixture in all our lives, and who lived next door. I arrived in Sheffield for the first term. That was when I met Ann. But when Cherry Blossom came to visit me one day, Ann just left and never contacted me again. She said it was plain to see we were in love, and anyone in the middle would only get hurt. We were of kindred spirits.

After that I returned in October, for just a few days as Aunty Bertha had died, I was so angry and sad. The way she acted when I was leaving, she seemed very happy and relieved, and although I felt she was happy for me, I felt suspicious; as if I would not see her in this life again; as if she wanted me out of the house to die; out of the way. I felt that she wanted me out of the way, so that I wouldn't see her suffer.

Soon after while I was at university both mother and father died, and that was when I buried this book at the bottom of the garden where they would sit late of an evening in summer, trying to turn the hillocks of Warwickshire into the green of hills that rose from the beaches up to the sky, where their everlasting greenness and terraces seemed like steps to heaven; where they would imagine twilight in the Caribbean when the satin sun would sit in a blaze of glory, and as night fell the moon glowed like an orb of satin, too. In this house where our joy was created and where they would end, in the garden where both mother and Aunty Bertha had planted onions, peas and peppers for their pepper pot because I knew the wilderness years were truly about to begin, and even Charlotte and Linda would die. The perfection in my world would collapse, and I would become the saddest person in this world.

That is why I buried this book as a time capsule to be read as future reference, because I could see forecasts of rivers of blood and the apocalypse to come, when love would be lost, where ugliness was beauty and beauty was ugliness, a world where even children would be forced to hate and despise goodness. It is a future that I see, but one which I am powerless to avert or defend against its march of challenges, which will stretch human endurance, emotions, and tolerance, far beyond the limits of love.

Chapter Nineteen

THERE ARE TWO TALES TO the story of the monkey on the crocodile's back crossing the river. In fact, some even say that it was on an alligator's back instead of a crocodile's back upon which the cheeky monkey sat. This version of the conversation went like this.

"Will you give me your heart, if I take you with wet feet across the river?"

"Yes, if you save my child from drowning."

"Under what sky?" the alligator sighed.

"Any sky, but I ask nothing for myself. I only wish my child to be born under a satin sun and die with a satin moon, shining overhead. As for my own death, I shall let you decide."

"I will take you across the great, green ocean of time." said the alligator.

"I know of the great ocean," the cheeky monkey replied. "And I know the colours of hope: red, green and gold is the rainbow."

"I am a mother myself." said the alligator. "I need my children to be fed, and for food, I must ask for your heart."

"You may have my heart, my liver, my kidneys, and my spleen. But spare my child. Promise me a nativity; send Gaspar, Melchior, and Balthasar to the water birth when my water breaks, so that the soul of this child I carry can be saved."

"Under what sky?" asked the alligator.

"As before, but make my death quick, when my water breaks, eat my body."

The alligator ate the mother and the child. But their spirits reside in me, I am the transformer of souls, and created of the self - same spirit as the first voice that strives; that exists under a yellow satin summer sky, lit by a harvest gold satin sun by day, and a full yellow moon by night, neither dimmed nor hidden; bringer of hope, rainbow - woman of redemption. And this is my version of the same story.

But before I begin my very own tale, let me remind you that I am dead; let me remind you also that the old Anancy storytellers say the crocodiles were abhorred by the heinous deeds of their alligator cousins, and labelled them barbarians. But the proverbs also say each devourer passes judgement, and their faith is to abjure their own acts of devouring and find catharsis in their own acts of human sacrifice.

But I am the ever-recurring Mako that dances on the streets of Nassau. Many holidaymakers have seen me; paid me tributes; taken photographs with me. Some only to realize that when they take their holiday snaps back home to New York to show off to their friends, that my picture is not there, or sometimes my picture is there, but theirs is not. And they have been warned beware the Mako of the islands. Many have disappeared, because they do not know the power of the spirits, and do not pay close attention. Some even offend by disbelief in our powers. Sometimes there is death in denial.

In my many lives, I am truly transformed. My name is Cherry Blossom, and I am a woman who have always demanded the impossible. I fly, change my human form, and live on fire. Being three dimensional, I am the spirit of the Mako with six- hundred and sixty - six different loas.

That afternoon I was seated on the largest, most expensive tomb stone in the cemetery at Camp Hill, and I saw them walking down the hill. Joseph and a fair, pale - skinned girl, whom I had seen before wandering among the graves. She always looked lost, as if she was trying to get out of the cemetery but could never find the right path. As small as the space were, she would wander around, but always seemed to find herself back where she started. But that afternoon she followed behind him, and I caught up with them at the bus stop. We boarded the bus together, but I lost them at Halley Green, next to the college.

I knew she was a strange spirit: she had died six months before, burnt to ashes with her mother and her child. Although no actual remains were found, the girl's father a devout Pentecostal had forced Mr Jenna, the Asian landlord to scoop up what remains were in the property, which he had placed in a coffin for burial. At nights there were several sightings of this beautiful young girl, sometimes alone, and at other times with the mother and child wringing her hands at the roadside. Sometimes, even begging passers-by.

Wandering around that afternoon, I found them at a house in the area and the smell of burning was so strong that I dared not enter the house. The scent of burning burnt flesh, plastic materials, animal, vegetable, and synthetics was so strong that I rushed from the area.

It was the first and last time that I had ever been near a furtive spirit, and her entire aroma was so powerful that I gave up trying to save him that afternoon, because she was very powerful medicine, and I had only a little time before I returned to my world of darkness and light.

Since then, she has been hovering near our houses and has influenced him on several occasions to abandon his family. He has been leaving home off and on for years and still cannot figure out the true reasons for his desertions of his family, and sometimes total disregard for people who love him. And he thinks he knows everything about life, death, the after - life, the pre—life and what he terms the real world—the world of reality. But in truth he knows nothing. All that first voice has told you—that is what I call him—first voice, among other names. All that first voice has said are the tails of flipped coins. This is the head which I have won on every conceivable occasion.

Chapter Twenty

THE AFTERNOON I SLEPT IN first voice's bed; our fates were sealed. The pact had been sealed and signed forever. He did not know it, then, but I was not there when he watched me sleeping, or else we would not have died together.

It was a consanguineous marriage: an eternal tying of the knot, because many of our family did that in the past, until they became human. We used to say the meat is sweetest when it is closer to the bone. Therefore, it did not stir a thought in me when Charlotte married Geremel. And that afternoon Aunty Bertha picked me for first voice. That day when she said to me:

"Go and sleep in his bed if you want him to love you more 'an anything in this earth. Mek im find you asleep in his bed; be his little golden girl – his likkle darlin'; go ahead girl."

So up I went, I was so sleepy, beating cake for them to bake. My arms were so tired. We spent long, lazy, and hazy weekends preparing cakes and curries for christenings, funerals, and weddings. On Saturdays we cooked spicy mutton soups, and even mutton haters ate this soup. Cooked with sweet cassava, sweet potatoes, carrots, green bananas and dumplings, it was irresistible. Sunday was also cake baking day, because we would beat and mix the ingredients of the cake on Thursday and set the fusions to soak. Cooking soups on Saturdays, afforded time to concentrate on baking.

In those days only the loose living among us ever attempted parties that were strictly for pleasure. We celebrated not hedonism, but rites of passage. That was the most distinct difference between us and the good—for—nothing—people that my father Blades, and godfather Archippus, and later Rudy and Joseph began to entertain as acquaintances; and later to make family ties more dissolute, Rudy would become unequally yoked, and would be called "a rent a man," like a bull pastured out for breeding a certain type of beef. He would drink himself senseless. And more alarming, he had renewed the fascination with fire that he had as a child and started lighting small fires in the garden at home or in respective family homes when he visited.

When criticized, stubbornness and alcohol would feed his paranoia which seemed to have led him to the belief that Linda had committed suicide and abandoned him and their four children, having taken the eldest down to the deep with her in the land down under called Australia. His words; not mine. His two weaknesses fuelled his disillusionment.

Chapter Twenty-One

THERE WERE NO DOUBTS IN our minds that Linda fully intended to return to us after holidaying in Australia. In her decision to travel she had fought off the resistance of her parents who were dead set against the trip. She had also put to rest the deliberations of Rudy, and pressure from our side, except, Aunty Bertha. Although we had on our side professional exiles, the majority saw her choice of holiday as one of the two places on earth that was too far, and far too remote to go on any trip and, certainly too hostile to settle, and leave after five years.

Rudy had wanted to go to America, meaning the United States, and we were all familiar with America as the centre of the world. Another stumbling block that stopped our side's consent was that we fully intended to leave England soon; it was our fifth year, and the stay was over; time was running out; we missed the sun, and relatives were clamouring to leave, because our parents—all the big people had said five years. Five years in England and we will come home; their parents were home in the sun getting worried about children being born abroad; because some even said the rising tide of Anglomania was a trick to steal our sunshine, and sell it to America, meaning the United States, and Canada.

Unknown to us at the time, Linda's interest in wanting to see the other side of the globe had been sparked off by a postcard that she had been given by the postman years before. This was intended for the new neighbours at twenty - five Marmalade Lane; they lived at twenty - seven. She had witnessed the postman's frustration as he tried to fit the property, still with the for sale sign up, with the name he was fumbling to spell. He could not see how the surname Solomon matched the picture postcard of Sydney Harbour, and a remote village in the backwater of Warwickshire.

Linda had seen so many people come and go, and could not decide who the new owners were, and still no one had moved into the property. There was more confusion because none of the tradesmen working on the house would engage her in conversation when she tried to hand over the postcard. She ended up putting it in her treasure box with her dolls and playthings that she had been bought over the years and thought nothing of it.

In July nineteen sixty - four a parcel arrived at Uncle Jeroboam's house in Handsworth. It was an unusual parcel as it was a rectangular object about eighteen by twenty inches, and flat. It was stamped Victoria, Australia, and when it was unwrapped it contained a framed poem, with a picture of an American president, and a postcard of Sydney Harbour.

The opening stanza of the poem read:

> Death will come soon or late
>
> And no one could anticipate
>
> So tragic an event
>
> That overtook the life of our president …

The poem continued in six more quatrains and was very respectful of the late president. The postcard read "Nice day here in A, tying me kangaroo down sport. Uncle Dada."

There was talk about Uncle Dada, who wrote poems and fancied himself a lady's man and a painter. He was a Levy and had light brown hair, a Bustamante swagger and the brinkmanship and other worldliness of Norman Manley. How did he end up in Australia?

We learned that he had left Mandeville having been invited to Victoria by one of his rum drinking soldier friends, whom he had fought alongside in the great war. During countless Sunday dinner discussions, we learned that Uncle Dada had married an Aborigine woman by the name of Dell, much against the caution of his host, and the authorities. Aunty Bertha was always silent, while one brother described their mother's brother as a Nevis Sephardic, the other a belligerent Cayman islander.

Piecing together this puzzle of a man, we learned that in his stint in the great war, he flew fighter planes, fought American soldiers in pubs when on leave because he dated white women. Out boxed Aussies; made friends with them; fought them to a standstill; got drunk with them, played, and argued about cricket. He had on several occasions settled with his fists curt and unguarded remarks about his mixed heritage, which was not always apparent to those who went only by his complexion. The soldiers and officers of the West Indies Regiment, and all his Aussie, and Asian friends called him "Alligator Man". How were they to know his implied namesake, the species had become a delicacy to the locals and had long since become extinct?

During the fifties Uncle Dada had spent most of his time between the Levy Estate on Grand Cayman and the pimento farms in Mandeville. He had picked up this lavish lifestyle after the war as he had lived most of his life, until nineteen sixty when preparations were being made to return the islands to the crown after three hundred years as part of the legislature of Jamaica.

While there were troubles brewing in the mixed island homes; turmoil in the houses of assembly, the soul searching led to too many casualties, one of which was the future of the small community scattered inter islands. Until then Benjamin Mandelbaum Bertram Levy had not a care in the world. This, however, was about to change.

After witnessing violent political rallies on business trips to Kingston, fed up with political brinkmanship, his cousin Josiah Mandelbaum, who was never devout in the past, stopped eating lobster, shrimps and other crustaceans, excluding crabs - because, in his own words - he could never allow himself to stoop so low as to consume a creature with an obsessive appetite for excrement and carrion. He who had once driven his servants to distraction when they refused him chicken not reared in the yard, in a penned in chicken coop, suddenly began to insist on kosher; grew a beard; began wearing sackcloth and, then out of the blue, emigrated to Israel.

Chapter Twenty-Two

THIS WAS THE CONTRADICTORY LEVY trait; a strain that veered between commerce and belief almost all the entire way through life; common sense capacity for things secular, and passion for faith: complex layers of emotions that oscillated between hope and desolation; joy and despair; construction and destruction. But overall, was the innate capacity to invite and the incapacity to resist temptation.

The eldest son of Martha Levy, as if waking from pleasant dreams of home had awakened from the restful calm of sleep and had walked into a real-life nightmare. A situation not entirely unlike his last real nightmare when he tottered on the edge of a cliff, fighting the balance of gravity not to trip and fall over the edge.

For Uncle Jeroboam, the romantic dispositions of his mother's family were interesting, perhaps, even at times unexpectedly profitable, but overall, led to leaving important things for others to do while they followed their impetuous, and personal agendas, which might be myriads of changes, all expected to be accommodated and completed in one day: twenty-four hours being too short for their impetuosity.

Three months to the day the first package arrived from Victoria, another package arrived from Uncle Dada. This contained three photographs of himself, his new wife Dell and their three-year-old daughter called Martha. The whole family were stricken with this Australasian with smooth black skin, and hair with droplets of curls that reminded them of beautiful dreadlocks that fell to her shoulders, and she looked feisty, too. The child like Siobhan, had bright copper skin, with a tinge of her father's fairness, and many remarked that she would grow into one of those strawberry complexioned girls that Ian Fleming wrote about in his travel book to Jamaica.

There were rumours that when the package containing the letter and photographs were opened, Uncle Jeroboam had his eureka moment, and shouted from the bath.

"Bluudclaat!"

Over the next weeks the photographs of Uncle Dada and his immediate family became very popular. Printed copies were made, especially as the originals were so often handled that they were becoming dog eared, having been passed around at dinners, funerals, christenings and on every family occasion. Relatives from far and wide began visiting either to have a look or to order their own copies of the famous, Uncle Dada, celebrity photographs.

One evening Uncle Charlie arrived at the house to collect his copy of the photograph; he too wanted it framed and hung on the wall of his living room. His elder brother gave him his ordered copy, which was already framed. Then apparently, they had dinner. During dinner Rudy arrived with a letter from Linda. He had read and reread this letter several times and with every read his mind became more confused. Aunt Bernice was besides herself for the sadness of her son, who was going through a crisis of identity, which she always feared might be inevitable.

Charlie, her young brother in - law had also arrived with a letter from Santiago. This was in Spanish. Like all Solomon women she was a tower of strength and sat bemused as her husband struggled with the translation. He must have been relieved because when she held out her hand, he obediently handed over the letter. It transpired that Santiago had also left the estate in Grand Cayman in the hands of its workers, or to fend for itself, and had also emigrated to Australia.

"Bluudclaat!" He exclaimed and continued eating his rice and peas.

Uncle Jeroboam pondered whether the three had gone totally mad, or whether their displays of infamy indicated a type of adulation that had prompted his uncle to go travelling.

The Grand Cayman estate, together with the pimento farms in Mandeville had passed to the keep of Santiago, a Cuban cousin who was just as breezy headed as the other two relatives. He held a similar attitude to life, and was a swashbuckling Levy, and exhibited similar traits from committed dissoluteness to awe—inspiring and unexpected piety. When he got drunk, he cried for his own sins, and the sins of others.

The search for such conflicts and comparisons had influenced Linda's search for adventure; that had bearing on her decision to travel to Australia, and which must have intrigued her to keep up correspondence with the puzzle of a man such as Uncle Dada. The world changed completely when she left for Victoria soon after the arrival of the second package. Uncle Jeroboam was astounded; my godfather was amazed, Aunty Bertha kept silent when the family finally learned the connections.

Chapter Twenty-Three

ALL HAD NOT BEEN WELL between Rudy and Linda for a long time. She longed for romance; he dreamt only of it but could never make time for it. In the end they both agreed to have a trial separation, but it was Linda's idea, because Rudy wanted the situation to remain unchanged as he felt that a ring on a woman's finger meant that she had no other choice than to put her husband and family first, and ignore her own hopes, and desires, and even totally disregard her basic instincts.

Within a fleeting period, we were all shocked and dismayed at the decay, and of Rudy's deterioration after she left. Bernice his mother could not believe that their young love which began in earnest, could have become so irreconcilably strained; so sad; so irreconcilably old. That like a withered rose consumed by time, the once flourishing, blossoming, young love, became worn; and in the twinkling of an eye, had slowly withered and died. And he was a pyromaniac, who made her frightened of what he might do to the house in which they lived.

But in earnest Rudy lovable as he was, had too many faults for any woman to survive his belaboured love. He always struck me as one of those men that could never embrace criticisms, challenges, or flexibility. And then he loved lighting matches, holding them against the box and watching them burn. Then he would strike another one. His blue eyes dazed and looking into the flame. Those inflexible attitudes might be ironed out with patience and strength, but the delirium tremens showed signs of constant dilution of the grey matter of the brain; daily wear and tear that had become the new norm; and he refused to acknowledge that he was in urgent need of attention, treatment and, even, repair.

Rudy was a carpenter in Walsall and held down his job for years until he hit the bottle. He seemed not able to discriminate between beers, shots, shorts, or spirits. In due course, Linda had changed, because she had detected a dependence on alcohol to hold down his job. She blamed her father for introducing him to beers, which she maintained was responsible for his diabetes, because of the combination of yeast and sugar.

However, there were combinations of many defaults that placed the marriage at risk. As so often the case with addiction, Rudy argued through minefields of denials. He blamed sawdust from his job for his failing health; arguments with Linda which he claimed added to his stress, made him depressed so then he had to drink; not drinking enough water; not eating enough salads. Any excuses that he could lay his hands on were trumped up as justifications for his dependency.

The hangovers made him lethargic, dehydrated, and irritable; he developed irritable bowels and blamed it on her cooking; her inability to strain the soap off the washing up. The food she cooked gave him constipation; the salads, too green, gave him diarrhoea, and when the children cried or played too loudly that gave him splitting headaches and increased the throbbing pains of his migraine.

The final straw came for Linda when he started drinking the "dog's hair". Secretly, Aunty Bertha had advised her that she must leave her nephew; my mother, and godmother, who were never far behind my god aunt's interventions gave her holiday spending money, and later it transpired even helped with the passage to Australia, where they all felt was safe enough distance from Rudy. They expected her to return after three months and kept in touch by monthly letters. Later the men would deem these actions as direct challenges to their authority, but when they used that word to my models of womanhood, the retorts were:

"What authority? Whose authority? Who give you authority?"

Eventually, even aunty Bernice admitted that they had done the right thing because Rudy discovered other vices. He spent time with a new woman in Willenhall; spent his money at bookies; visited gambling houses and would leave the four children with family members every weekend and frequented blues parties in London, Wolverhampton, Nottingham, and of course, his own pitch in Handsworth.

Chapter Twenty-Four

OUR CLEFT IN THE ROCK was not Alum Rock, not Saltley, nor Wolverhampton, but Handsworth. It was there we showed strength, versatility; solidarity; self-reliance, and revolution. It was there in times when we needed refuge. It was where we opened our first shops and first two dance halls: the Rio and the Santa Monica.

Those of us who lived on the outskirts looked on Handsworth with mixed blessings: for all it was a place to run in times of trouble; for some it was a place where only horrific events happened. Yet, all were tainted for its, supposedly, violent reputation and the links they shared with it.

On three separate occasions I saw a man spilled like Cain his own brother's blood who bled to death. The gratuitous violence turned inward upon the community, based on the devaluation of black lives in the wider world and dominant culture. And yet, I saw other men risk a cut to stop the fights. Crowds gathered, not to watch and be entertained, but to stop the combatants from spoiling their fun and they did this with shouts of "Enough" for that was the liturgy of forbearance.

Invariably, life overtook us, violence came to us as if out of the blue. I recall one such incident. It was a Thursday in June and I had just left college. That very week preparations were being made for another wedding. Aunty Bernice and my mother had moved the preparations to Handsworth. But mischief was a foot in the shape of Charlotte, who by appearances many thought was happily married as she held down a responsible career.

Charlotte had been married off to Geremel five years before at sixteen. Aged twenty-one she was now the mother of three children: Reuben and Benjamin were twins, and their baby sister Leah, who was born three months prematurely. They seemed happy and well looked after children, and their parents had a comfortable life, and lived in a comfortable home. Charlotte was a state registered nurse, and Geremel a Capstan machinist at a local factory in Perry Bar.

Nobody knew exactly what time he came back into Charlotte's life. I went into Birmingham one Saturday afternoon with her. We were walking down the ramp from the Bull Ring when someone crept up behind us and put their hands over her eyes. I looked around and it was Boy. Charlotte purred like a kitten and chuckled like a young girl; she was so excited that her body was trembling, and she moved her spine in a rocking movement as if she was shivering, and she shouted his name and laughed with glee.

"What happening girl?" he said, dropping his hands around her neck, kissing her on the cheeks.

He looked at me. "Hello Cherry, baby. Good to see you."

"Cool" I replied.

"Good!" he said.

Then he turned to her. "How has it been, baby girl?"

"You know how it is." she replied.

He walked alongside her, with his right arm encompassing her shoulders. She glanced to her right and, looking at him askance her lips parted as they made eye contact. I looked sideways and saw the intensity of their body language.

"You let me down, last week." she said.

"I called you, but you didn't answer. You let me down."

"Why didn't you call back?"

"Let's meet at Santa Monica, weekend. You just tell the door, you're my guest, and they'll let you in."

Charlotte chuckled. "You just side stepped my question."

"You said not to phone the house, remember?"

We had reached the end of the ramp. He squeezed her arm gently, smiled, and turned back. We walked on, but I could sense the need in her to look back; to look back in his direction, but perhaps, fearing that like Lot's wife the knot of their newly found love might break, or that she might turn into a pillar of salt. A woman forced to love outside of herself into a marriage that was doomed from the beginning, and that in attempting to turn the clock back, too much time had been lost. That through no fault of her own, her body and her soul cried out for the one she loved; the one that was her choice. And now she had, through her own fault, succumbed to temptation. That in truth she had become a fallen woman.

Saturday came. The club was a whitewashed building that stood at the intersection of Soho and Villa Road. The air was cool in the midsummer night as we stepped out of the taxi.

Once in the cool air I felt a breezy excitement, with the bright lights from the lamp posts shining so brightly. The neon lights from the club persuaded you to enter its world.

The colour spectrum, arranged in the twelve tribes of Israel, streamed from the whitewashed walls; this with the colours of the rainbow spelt your name. The music persuaded you that this was a place where love was found, or if love ever failed, you were compensated with a sense of belonging.

Designated the temple of sin, good Christian children, driven to and from church, leaned out of car windows to catch the words of a song that wafted on the breezy air, subconsciously, committing to memory, alliteration, a refrain, a simile, a metaphor that remained fixed in the mind, that marked Santa Monica as one of the places they must go before they die. The temptation to one night enter its doors was always there.

Charlotte was besides herself, dressed in flowing orange, which complemented my blue outfit, she looked a gift, ready and waiting to be unwrapped by long, delicate, and musical fingers. Tempted. An inexplicable magical glow illuminated the intersection that marked it off as a special spot and imparted a sense of wonder to the breezy night as the song floated on the air, and even the streetlights gave a magical glow to the entire street.

And I heard it. And Charlotte heard it, too. A favourite tune, we had heard in passing this place of sin that pastor had called the congregation of the damned. It was playing, and the words spoke to my heart, as if that song had been written just for me. And I looked around at Charlotte, and she was wiping the tears away from her eyes, when the singer sang:

> "Weep, oh, willow weep, let me hear your song, so that my
> soul will be filled with joy…"

Chapter Twenty-Five

"WE'RE PLAYING AUSTRALIA", UNCLE JEROBOAM said, and turned up the radio. He stood listening to the rest of the news.

He was passing through the kitchen, and came over to play with my hair, and insisted that I should share the cake beating with Charlotte, and intended bride, because I always seemed to be the one sole cake beater killing myself for the rest.

"Some of your peers have small, small gratitude; and most of them have none." he said before he walked away.

"I wonder who upset him now?" said mother.

"No one. He just throwing word." said godmother.

The minute he walked out the door, Aunty Bertha turned off the radio, and hushed the others by putting her finger to her lips.

Henrietta was getting married. The elders had come to our house to organize the bonds and prepare the cake. Uncle Charlie came in from round the back, scolding. We could hear arguments coming from that direction.

"We told her it was stupid."

"But her parents met with the man already, and he willing to come to church, and get married like we do, in a church.

"This is madness; this is not going to work."

"Of course, it's going to work. This Indian will full her up of coolie pickney. Look how them breed a ready."

"Don't go there. Don't."

The door closed, and we could hear their voices muffled, but still in argument.

Godmother looked at my mother and winked. "They're up to something. I bet they lettin' us go through the motion, and as time come, they intend to stop the wedding."

"I wouldn't put it beyond their wicked hands. But look at it this way, Henrietta is a beautiful girl. She is best with her own." And she started to sob.

"I don't know what will become of us." said aunty Bernice.

"Either way, these are drastic measures. Think what that will do to the poor girl. Charlie and Divine let those girls off too easy. They spare the rod and spoil the child. Like they don't understand the teachings of Jesus." said Aunt Marva.

"They know whether we approve of the match or not, we will back the girls; they are women like us." said godmother.

"Suffer the little children to come unto me, said the good Book, and these Hindus have more than one Gods; they worship stone and animals." aunty Marva replied.

The doorbell rang, and I went to open it. Charlotte, Rashida, and Esme entered, filled with excitement at the prospect of another wedding. They went to the living room and continued haggling over what colour dresses to wear as bridesmaids. It was time to beat the samples of cakes and set the ingredients for next year. I returned to the kitchen.

It was late autumn and with the onset of winter, everything needed strict organisation. Since one of the conditions of Henrietta marrying Ram meant they had to have a church wedding. There would be a Christian ceremony. The women in the family thought this was the only way that Henrietta should be allowed to marry a pagan. As far as they were concerned, she had kept herself pure in heart, and her body free of transgressions of the flesh. They applauded themselves that she was going to her husband's bed with the perfect purity of a chaste and unsoiled Christian woman.

Uncle Jeroboam came back into the house, walked straight to the living room, and brought the haggling bridesmaids to work. He looked at me annoyed and said:

"Didn't I tell you to watch these lazy bones. Mind, you know. They will kill you off before your time. All they do is make up they self. There is more to marriage than the marriage bed, and a pretty face."

We were all trying to cope with his new attitude since his uncle ran off to Australia and started making new babies. There was now a new sense of urgency in his life, and he was always writing letters to Bermuda to his parents, or answering letters from Uncle Dada, or the Cuban idiot, as he called Santiago. He remarked, scathingly, that Santiago was a saltwater alligator.

We had no idea what he meant until a letter came from Uncle Dada late November when the snows were harsh, and the winter winds blistering cold. It was so cold that the family rarely saw one another and had to communicate mostly by telephone. The summer had been good to us, autumn warmer than usual, but winter knocked us for fours and sixes. The winds were harsher than before, and all the talk was about going home, the bitter cold. Prayers hastened the glory of spring. The ice was thawing, but not quickly enough.

The contents of the mystery letter were out when the coldness abated, or shall I say, the snow plough was able to clear the icebergs from the roads and the grit safe enough to drive. They met at my parents' house in Sutton Coldfield, which was becoming neutral ground as there were so many crises happening between the Solomon family at the time. We were less involved in the Levy and Solomon rivalries, and therefore, considered neutral, and being neither in one camp nor the other, everyone except, King Jaja, respected my parents' refusal to judge.

It was so cold that going to church was a long and distant memory, as now families held prayer meetings at home. Coming up to Christmas, though, the snows abated, and we received our guests. The house became the centre of the Christmas celebrations, too, with relatives coming and going, and Christmas lights surrounding the front and back of the house.

One day we had snowball fights, and everybody joined in, with each man for himself. It was riotous and a complete shamble. But everyone loved it, apart from godmother, mother and Aunty Bertha. They disliked the numbness and the cold. When pushed they ran back into the house and refused to take part. And those who stayed out laughed.

During that time my father Blades seemed to have settled into the role of confidante to Uncle Jeroboam, and they spent time in the garden together, and were always in deep conversation. The only other person who was involved in these private conferences was my godfather. Aunty Bertha seemed overjoyed that the triumvirate - as she nicknamed them - were sorting out the business of how things are done. And godmother said they had the handle on how things work, and not the blade, and they laughed because my father's name was Blades, and he always dressed well and looked sharp as a razor.

Oddly enough, Rudy and Geremel turned up at the house one Thursday. Rudy was completely sober, but Geremel was unsteady on his feet, and his speech was slurred. All his talk was about Charlotte, his children, and Boy. He was in the kitchen in tears when Aunty Bertha said to him:

"Why you not seeing your children with Charlotte?"

He seemed taken aback by this and could not find an answer, so he just mumbled, incoherently, and sat down. Rudy went to the fridge and poured him a drink of ginger and sipped the tea he had made for himself.

"Why are you giving him cold ginger when you give you self-hot tea?" she said.

"Because he is drunk taunty. Look at him: drunk, drunk, drunk!"

"I could see that!" she said flatly.

"Don't worry 'bout me too tough taunty." Geremel groaned.

"He'll be all right." Rudy jumped to his defence.

She turned to me, smiled, and played with my hair.

"Cherry mek your cousin some hot ginger, please."

"Yes, Aunty Bertha." I said and made him some hot tea.

When he took it. He took the first sip and belched loudly.

"Sorry." he said putting his hand to his mouth, and tried to smile, but he was too embarrassed to smile properly.

"You have wind. Think of what is coming out at the other end. Disgusting!" she said.

"Everybody has wind." Rudy said.

"Of course; but there is good wind, and bad wind. Good food gives you good wind; bad food gives you bad wind. It's simple as that. Bad and evil thoughts give you a bad and evil life. Good is best, always."

Rudy suddenly seemed intrigued and began to warm to her advice. She looked at them both like the nurse she was, as if looking at their ailment. Just then Joseph came into the house from the cold garden; kicked his shoes off and ran up the stairs. She looked at me.

"Why your eyes always follow Joseph like that?"

"He's always running in the house." I spoke.

She looked me over with disbelief and turned to the other two.

"Dates and pineapple are good for wind. They break down the acids in the body that give bad wind. Most times good wind doesn't smell, and nearly good wind not so offensive. But bad wind…bah … bad wind, bad, bad, bad…"

The boys started to laugh, Aunty Bertha started laughing, too, and I suddenly could not help myself, and laughed out loud.

"And another thing, constipation give very bad wind: like something in there that can't get out: things piling up. Then you need a wash out once a month."

"Oh, I see, said Geremel."

"My ailment is the breast, and I been using good wind to fight it. We don't have no African hospital, so I going to lose one day. But we fighting it hard, and the hospital, too."

That was the first time we had heard her refer to her ailment. We had found Joseph crying round the back at Waterston one day, and he was so distraught that we felt sorry for him. He even had my sympathy, which was unusual because I had always wanted to be tough on him. But he was crying and could not stop the tears; we thought he was deluded when he insisted that Aunty Bertha was dying. This was seven years ago, and she was still with us. King Jaja had really been a blessing, and we were all grateful to him.

"And sometimes starve your ancestors of food, and sugar … even water, too. And silence is golden, remember that." she said.

The doorbell rang, and Joseph came bounding down the stairs to let in Jay, who came into the kitchen to greet everyone. Then they were off to the ice rink in Snow Hill to skate. Whenever Jay was around, we noticed that Joseph had no time for anyone. They went upstairs to listen to music; came down about half an hour later, and just left without saying goodbye.

Chapter Twenty-Six

"SO HOW MANY CHILDREN YOU have then?"

That was Uncle Jeroboam and my father. They had come in from the cold and had brought some of the fog in as the door opened. It circled the room momentarily and melted like candy floss expunged by the heat. Uncle Jeroboam and father were discussing the future of Charlotte and Geremel. Charlotte wanted a divorce because she said her husband had lied to her about his commitments in Jamaica. He had been sending money to girlfriends and had been in three different relationships before they were married.

Aged twenty-six, he was father to their three children; and four by three different relationships; two women from Jamaica and the other from Grand Cayman. He had seven children in all and wanted more. He had been pestering Charlotte to have more access to her bedroom, so they could try for a fourth, a fifth and may be, even a sixth.

There was a long, awkward pause. No one said a word. Aunty Bertha went to the stairs and called Raina, Henrietta, Rachael and Esme downstairs. They rushed down the stairs and entered the dining room. They sat down in the large spare settee.

"Yes. How many children in Grand Cayman? One or two? You might as well tell us the truth." said my father.

Geremel was dumbfounded. He fidgeted on his seat, wrung his hands, and began to crack his knuckles. The presence of us girls was making him even more embarrassed than if we weren't there.

"Answer the question!" Uncle Jeroboam insisted.

He rubbed his forehead as if attempting to smooth out the creases. Then he took off his hat and gave his bald pate a slow and prolonged rub, starting from his forehead to the back of his neck, and then to the front of the head, and closed his eyes.

Aunty Bertha looked at Geremel, sympathetically, then at her brother,

"I don't want to undermine what's going on here, but surely you both have the answer. As I understand it, husband here already had children before and lied to pastor, and now won't see the children unless their mother agrees to make more."

"I wasn't marrying pastor." said Geremel.

"But you lied to pastor; to Charlotte, and even to Divine." said Uncle Jeroboam. Then he caressed his forehead. "You know you lied to pastor and your marriage is over. You drink too much rum. Charlotte want back the keys. You have to leave the keys."

Rudy had been shaking his legs nervously throughout the exchanges sprang to his feet. "Excuse me, but I can't see where all this is leading."

"Si down you punky," said Uncle Charlie. He stood before him as he tried to reach the door. "Si down. That why the saltwater crocodile dunga Cayman got you wife a ride he back lek a monkey."

Everybody started laughing; all except Rudy who walked back to the stool and sat down with a shocked look of wonderment on his face.

"See, we wus coming to you soon. But you jump the gun. We word is law in this family." said Uncle Charlie.

"Ehem," said godfather. Mr Man. Ongly one rooster crow unda fe we roof."

"Children. Children." said Aunty Bertha. And she looked at godmother and mother. They looked back at her and smiled, and all three recited in unison:

"Yes papa. Behave yourselves, or licks will fly. When you in this house you not ina Inglan."

Chapter Twenty-Seven

T HAT REMARK COULD NOT HAVE been more accurate to describe our anomie. We were divided spirits. Everyone had been asleep. We were not aware when our parents realized that they had brought us sleeping walking through the back door of heaven, but as the first revelations hit us for six, we had no culture to get even; we just got mad and rebelled.

It was that similar trait of spirit that got men like Uncle Dada and his regiment into trouble. After the war, they had to be disbanded because they had welded themselves into a martial arts fighting machine, having designed an exceptional fighting style by linking arms, and kicking, then breaking free, and reassembling, as disparate parts of the machine reformed to ambush, confuse, and bludgeon the enemy: "the Yankees gone, West Indians take over now" so went the chant as they clashed with the sons of Uncle Sam at local pubs in London. They called their fighting style "the robot."

"Hey nigger!"

Wha' you say. Wha you bloodclaat say?"

"Hey nigger!"

"Raas man!"

"Hey nigger!"

"You tink you is a saga boy?"

And in the back pocket was a razor. Mighty Sparrow had sung "ten to one is murder."

The demobbing of the regiment began with haste when a corporal had shot up a London pub. Uncle Dada had been to the pub the day before and the bartender had refused to serve him. The next day he returned carrying a long sack which he placed on a table at the back of the pub. The bar lady refused to serve him.

He walked back to the table. Pulled the rifle from the sack, and targeted the lights in the ceiling, with well-chosen expletives. This had locals in the pub shuddering with fear, others in fits, and stitches of laughter.

Sympathetic to his trauma some kind soul bought him a drink, and paid a month's deposit that ensured his membership of his local pub. He lived there for three months, and when he was returning home, he went to say farewell and bought all his friends each a drink. Uncle Dada was an unusual character. That kind person was Telford, his Aussie friend, who had invited him to live in Australia.

Unafraid they had stared death and failure in the face more than once and were men that struggled with themselves. Our men, on the other hand, were being brought up to acquiesce to our fate of uncertainty, when we needed to be sure. It was as if coming to England, nobody expected to die. But whom does death overlook? No one.

There were even more changes as we all tried to adapt to the new realities that were sweeping the host country. From snippets of conversation, we overheard stirrings that hinted that all was not well within our homes that ought to have been the epitomes of Christianity. We had only become children of the fog. Through which our eyes had to pierce beyond, so we could see the sun, satin, or trapped by clouds belched from chimneys, and always looking for the moon, satin, purple, grey or otherwise, but mostly, all we saw were grey skies.

People like Charlotte, Henrietta, and Joseph developed "don't care" attitudes with talk of reducing the age of majority from twenty-one to eighteen, we saw this as the right to resist the exacting discipline of our parents. That was the talk. But we had been exercising our rights long before staying out all night had become the norm. Night life was the pull.

Sunday bests became Saturday night bests.

The blues parties drew us like moths to light bulbs. Children began to fall asleep at classes in schools. Christian children especially, like opposing magnets, could no longer resist the pull of opposite attraction. The catacombs of night life: abandoned houses; houses newly renovated; rented halls, the Rio, and especially, the Santa Monica, once temples of sin, became palaces of redemption.

Charlotte and I went to the Santa Monica on several occasions. We came across newly reinvented words such as "rave" and "bleach," "cool," "bangarang," "ramjam," "rock steady," "wabeen." People from aspiring homes left the sobriety of the living rooms with their crochet flowers, crochet tablecloths and ornate plastic flowers and learned to dance like the children of the congregation of hell. Our parents despaired but accepted our life style of shebeens and blues parties.

There was a banana tree right of the entrance which gave the illusion that we were home; towering far right of it stood a hawthorn. There was the uncanny feeling of make – believe as we walked through the black wrought iron gates and the words of the song we'd heard playing from afar, became clearer.

This was one of the best songs that I had heard my godfather play on Iron Sound. The song was called "Loving Pauper." The singer's name was Dobbie Dobson, and by our standard it was what we called a "tune," meaning it merited rewind, at least, three times.

We were fish caught dangling on hooks. The music carried the words, and both floated like magic on the air; the words like the sweet taste of honeycomb honey melting on the tongue, flooding the palate, and he weakened my legs. I would learn later at university that this was metaphysical poetry, with an Argument.

> I am not in a position, to maintain you,
>
> The way that you're accustomed to
>
> Can't take you out to fancy places,
>
> Like other fellows that I know can do
>
> I'm only able to romance you,
>
> And make you tingle with delight,
>
> Financially I'm a pauper
>
> But when it comes to loving am all right…

We had heard stirrings of this song play in passing cars, its music drifting on the midland air. Pulling up outside or passing venues, when being driven to or from church, we had danced in our seats to its lyrics; only to be shouted down to stop, stay still, and behave ourselves. But still enthralled by the fleeting pitch of its hypnotic rhythms, and the ingenuity of its tone - the argument, we had all agreed in casual conversations with our friends that its sound had sealed its version as a "tune." Myriads of times, when our parents' cars pulled up at the traffic lights outside the Rio, we had hoped the lights could have taken a little longer to change so that we could hear more bars of it. Then to hide our disappointment, in an uncanny way of self - denial, we had dismissed its attraction as by far too vivid, and therefore, perhaps, it just played on our imagination because it was forbidden. Yet there we were living the experience of it all, with the music fluttering on the wind like the fragile and multicoloured wings of a bird of paradise beating the air. The words, together, with its haunting, pulsating polyrhythms, seem to open your heart out completely, and scramble your mind.

This they would have us deny, as if we had died and gone to heaven as if all the rough diamonds we were England had purified. They drove us hither and thither; frightened us with talk of damnation, and the fires of hell; washed us soaking wet in the blood of Jesus; immersed us in his sweat; forced and taught us to deny existence of that other self. Yet flooded our limbs with music and, like their parents before them fought the contradictions of their lives.

And, like frightened somnambulists we fought shadows and ourselves in our sleep, we sleepwalked. Unlike our grand - parents before them they refused to admit, ugly though we were, we had the music; that even in the womb, like they we had moved embryonic limbs to it, for the devil's music had seduced our souls. There was the rebel in us that not even the red blood of Jesus Christ would stain.

With his arms around my waist, I laughed. I cackled; I swooned. I swore by God and all his good angels that if I could find my Othello, have him redeemed; banished from his jealous rages his Iago. That if even hell should find me such a man. I would willingly give my heart, soul, body, and mind to him—as I would any man that could sing such sweet words - or even a man that could appreciate the intelligence of such a mind that could write and sing such sweet, sweet, and tender words as if they were meant just for me.

Chapter Twenty-Eight

THE LIGHTS WENT OUT. THE music stopped. There were mutterings and murmurings. There was the sound of a scuffle; people fighting at the back of the dance floor; then the disturbance died down. The music started up. The lights went on again. Then there was the sound of another scuffle breaking out, with voices raised in anger. The music started up again, but you could still hear people shouting; others arguing, still others remonstrating. The lights went on.

Suddenly the music came to a halt, and all the lights flickered out; then flickered on again. Then went out; someone screamed. The MC's voice bellowed in remonstrations; a single shot rang out and ricocheted somewhere. A woman's voice screamed, and I knew it was Charlotte's. I stirred, troubled in his arms.

"Stay close to me," he said and squeezed me closer. "I will protect you."

Against the wall where we had been dancing, very closely, perhaps, too closely, he covered me with his body, and kissed my mouth as I tried to scream away the pain, because I knew she was hurt, and wanted to run to her; to put my arms about her and take her from that dreadful place.

"Clear de place," someone shouted, "Dance ova an' done."

"We have a casualty here," said a female voice.

I heard Charlotte's voice screeching. It was subdued, as if she did not have enough air in her lungs so her voice to bring out the pain. He held my hands in a grip and pulled me towards the back of the dance floor, and I saw her seated on the floor. Between her screeching and her crying, she was babbling, incoherently, to a figure lying in a pool of blood. Boy's head was resting in her lap; you could see the whites of his eyes, blood poured profusely from the hole in his head, and another stream of blood was dripping from the middle of his chest. Charlotte was tearing pieces of her dress and tying them across his head in her frenzy to stem the flow of blood.

"Help me! Help me!" she begged.

Three people went forward and ripping pieces of cloth from their clothes, appeared to have stemmed the flow of blood from his head.

"The heart wound is hardest," one of her aiders said.

"Be careful; don't push too hard," said another.

"It's de MC," said another voice. "He is a good guy. Save him."

I stood motionless as if stuck to the spot as if the high heels I wore were made of glue. She was oblivious of me. And my friend, pulled me towards the exit. I followed, looking back. But when I reached the door, something primeval snapped, and all the years we had spent together came rushing to my mind, and the tears came in streams, running down my cheeks because I had been crying silently.

It was then I knew that this was not my Othello, my good angel. How could I abandon my kith and kin in her weakest moments?

"No!" I shouted. I pulled away and rushed back into the Rio.

Charlotte seemed exhausted. She looked pathetic, dishevelled, damaged and fallen from grace. The ambulance people had arrived and were giving oxygen to the gasping body of Boy. Then exhausted themselves they turned to her. One of the ambulance men said: "He's gone."

Charlotte wrung her hands, appeared to fight for air and let out a loud primal scream, somewhere between a howler and a bawling out, and burst into paroxysms of tears. A roll of thunder drummed outside, and we could hear the rain beating the tarmac like the feet of wild goats, or herds of wildebeest migrating; the swish of the water under the tyres of passing cars.

As I walked towards her, I felt lost; I felt hopeless. Then I realized that if I had all the power of this earth: all the mighty power in the world; all the faith that I could remove mountains, I would not be able to bring him back. I could not resuscitate his lungs with air, make the muscles of his heart move again, to ignite the fire of his life.

But I could remove her from this place, help her to flee the fog of desolation, and find refuge in any of our abiding places; that it would not matter which island if we were able to watch the sun go down in a blaze of glory and the moon rise in clouds that floated soft as satin. Once again, the wrath of God had with swords of blood thrown us from Eden. We never should have come to this place; breakers of the covenant we had embraced the mirages of Babylon. Suddenly the Rio had become a place fit only for the ungodly.

I gathered her up, putting her arms roundabout me, whispering to her as I would a child, and walked her out of that place. We walked to the taxi rank. When we got to my house, we stole up the stairs. She cleansed her dress, spent three hours in the shower, and slept in my bed that night, innocent as when we were children. It was usual after a blues dance or a big wedding on Saturday we always slept passed midday on Sunday, and I expected Charlotte to stay at our house until late evening. But when I awoke in the late morning she was gone.

Chapter Twenty-Nine

THE THIRD WEEK HAD PASSED so quickly that we could scarcely believe our loss. We were aggrieved. We had become insular as islands, not outward looking, that we acted and behaved like feral cats fighting for our small portion of territory; and that territory was the base of our forbidden city in which we relived individual memories of the subjects of our loss.

Everyone was locked into their own grief, we spoke of the beloved ones in short bursts of speech, and mostly incoherent utterances that to people outside of lockets of grief, what was said made no sense, as they were not part of the cycle of the language of bereavement.

Since losing my faith, I spent Sundays alone. I was not the only one. The young felt abandoned by God. We had been sleeping, and now awakened, and having to come to terms with our own mortality, we strayed from the crutch and illusion of faith, into the secular arms of apostasy where dreams and illusions brought comfort, and blind faith comfortable. Yet even then we must have known that we were in a place where hopes were dreams. Everlasting life as we demanded of God was never feasible. You had to die first to get to heaven. But the elders remained blinded. The loss of three of their children had aged our parents. But while they held fast to sustaining faith, we had no such grace against the treacherous misfortunes, betrayals of hope, the tough times of the age in which we lived, or the light - brigade - charge of destiny. Still feeling aggrieved, deserted, and bewildered, when home alone, I went over and over, and over again, in my mind, repeatedly in my mind, what I could have done to save the life of Charlotte.

It was Sunday afternoon and my parents had gone to church.

There was a sharp, flicking sound on my window; someone threw a stone strong enough to splinter the glass. It was a miracle that it did not crack. I looked out onto the streets, and it was Henrietta. The others had died, but pastor preached that God had saved her life as testimony to his power; that divine intervention had rescued her by rapture as if in a whirlwind; as he had lifted the old prophet Elias into the pearly gates, the blast had thrown her through the window of the house to walk away unscathed. But that her blessing had been a curse.

The spitting rain had wet her clothes lightly, but she was shaking from the chill as she entered the door. I was willing to let her back into my life and wished to clear the air. There had been too many castings off at the funeral, and none of us would accept loss easily; neither would we look at the situation for what it was worth. We who once spoke with one voice had lost our sense of purpose, since reason had walked out the door.

What exactly was she doing with Geremel that afternoon when Charlotte returned home? The majority of church members, spurred on by the hell fire and brimstone sermons of pastor Dingle believed that Charlotte had sinned, and paid for it with her life. For the wages of sin is death. Without any definitive understanding, they believed that she had been punished for hidden transgressions, articles of covenant that not only her, but the whole family had broken. The zealots openly claimed our misfortunes were signs that we had displeased God. Though, they offered nothing definitive just how we had sinned. But calloused by faith and its ignorance we accepted their derision.

We spoke at length over cups of bitter tea that Aunty Bertha had always used to prevent bad wind, and nibbled bits of pineapple lightly soaked in lime juice and Jamaican honey.

"Pray, tell," I said.

"I will tell you everything. I will only leave out details of the private things." she retorted.

I waited patiently for Henrietta to give account of herself. Hoping that her side of the coin would discount all the rumours that were flying about bright as kites on the wind.

Whether we were in Handsworth, Walsall or Waterston, as young girls my cousins Charlotte, Henrietta, Raina, Rachael, and I would sit out the back, counting the stars, and pointing up to the sky to find traces of a satin moon. I longed for those days. She smiled, sipped her tea, and began her story.

On arriving home Charlotte must have been certain that her house was burgled. The front door of the porch was barely on its hinges; the oak door to the house was severely damaged. In several places the marks on the wood showed signs that it had been hammered until the faïence of the door had split. Entering the hallway, she looked up the stairs and saw one of the children's wardrobes that had been brought out of their bedroom onto the landing.

Charlotte climbed the stairs stealthily; she could hear two people in conversation. That was Esme and Geremel; they had been seeing each other off and on, behind every one's back for many years. It must have started immediately after he came up from Jamaica to marry Charlotte. I told her about it in the first year, but she told Mama that I was jealous of her marriage and wanted Geremel for myself because he had good hair.

I was really surprised when she called me to the house, she was in tears. No words of sympathy could calm her. You know how Charlotte could be sometimes when she was hurt quick to the soul. Nothing would calm her. When I arrived at the house Esme and Geremel were in the bathroom and Charlotte was shouting at Geremel why he had broken the front door, moved the wardrobe onto the landing and scattered the whole library of books all over the floor.

""Why did you do it?"" ""Why did you do it?"" she was shouting.

""You think you smart. You happy go lucky girl. Married woman and professional… all de while carrying on with you dead man… heh.""

""Well, well, well."" Esme teased, hands on her hips.

""You Solomons too damn nuff; try to trap me just because I aint one a you."" said Geremel.

""Dey keep de rest of us out on a limb; we is the servant class fer dem. See how they keep Uncle Blades.""

I felt perturbed and stopped her, intervening.

"What did they mean by that?" I asked.

"So, you don't know; your parents haven't told you?"

"You know they don't tell us anything." I replied.

Henrietta became silent; we sipped our tea for a few minutes. Then she continued.

They went on arguing with Esme insulting our side of the family, and sometimes the whole family. She accused Uncle Jeroboam of taking her father Jerome for a fool, with accusations about the money and lands in Mandeville, Grand Cayman and Barbuda that the Solomons had never shared with anyone else. That they always thought of Blades as far family when he was really a Solomon, like them, as was Jerome.

"Oh, I see; now I understand why he spends so much time, nowadays talking a lot, like they are planning something." I spoke.

There was another awkward silence between us while we sipped our tea, and became totally distracted, and spoke about other things.

"But let me finish before they come."

She meant my parents, and whoever they would return with from church. I said nothing, but I imagined that it might be Uncle Jeroboam and her parents, and anyone else that might want to come along for Sunday lunch.

Charlotte was angry about those two in her house. It was clear that Geremel and Esme had broken into the house by sledge hammering the doors. All the doors had been battered. They laid in splinters on the floor. In the hallway the picture of Uncle Dada and his family; all the family pictures were like litter on the floor of the living room, and the containers for the takeaway food they bought laid scattered over the dining room. They had emptied the bins: piles of refuse, garbage, cans and empty bottles were thrown onto the kitchen floor.

It was clear to me that they had planned everything together; when I tried to support Charlotte, they turned on me with vulgar words, the likes of which I had never heard anyone in the family use, or any one in church use, and they kept on repeating those terrible words that the low-class people use all the time. It was shocking; I could not stand it anymore. So, I said to Charlotte, "Call the police!" But when Charlotte grabbed the telephone, the cord had been cut, and Geremel laughed, and said:

See; I thought of everything. Ah gwine fix you dis time."

"I told you when he came up, he was mine. Why did you listen to them? You too hard ears; you think you snap you fingers and the whole earth fall at you feet."

"Shut up crazy Esme and leave my sister alone!" I spoke.

Esme snarled; looked me from toe to head; then up and down and said:

""As fer you, Injun lova, mek we see if dey will allow you marry you lil Ijun man.""

""Leave my sister alone."" shouted Charlotte.

"Sista. Wha' you tink ah you wan ave sista. Me ha sista too; you know."

I looked at Henrietta, and tears were beginning to form in her eyes. I supposed they were tears for Charlotte, but not entirely.

I could remember her body language that day when Aunty Bertha had called them downstairs, questioned Geremel about his other children, and the lies that he had told pastor to get clearance to marry Charlotte. She had the same diffidence as Rudy, until my father challenged his attitude.

"Did you ever have feelings for Geremel?" I asked.

Well, I had seen Joseph, Rudy, Abdi, and all the boys play cricket at the park and round the back of our houses, and when anyone got fixed in the wicket and could see the ball so clearly that they could not bowl them out, they would fix a trap around the wicket, or stump them out. That was my strategy with Henrietta. I had stumped her. She bowed her head and tried to force a smile, but it was more like a sneer, because she averted her eyes.

"He forced me; and it only happened once." she said.

"That's incest." I spoke.

"The royals do it!" she reacted.

No; they don't!" I said, and added, "You are supposed to get married, otherwise it's a sin."

"He forced me one night when I went to the Rio, and I was in the dark jamboree corner, when someone pulled me to dance. It was that tune by Slim Smith that got me. I loved that song. And the place was dark and musky smelling, a clean musk, though. I always loved to dance that tune.

> From nowhere through a caravan
>
> Around the campfire light
>
> A lovely woman in motion
>
> With hair as dark as night
>
> Her eyes were like that of a cat in the dark ...

"Oh, my God. Sin you say. What a sweet, sweet, sweet sin. May the Lord have mercy on my soul. This person grabbed me, and I was lost; he rubbed and squeezed me from earth to heaven; took my body around the campfire light and back. Forgive me, I couldn't help myself. I was ashamed when the lights came on and I saw it was him."

"That's not what I heard; not entirely."

"I don't care. I am telling you the gospel truth, I swear. I'm a Levy, and oh, God, I am so weak to temptation!"

"Temptation is sin"

"What a sweet sin!"

"I see cousins dance like that with each other and they know it's not right."

"To me it was always just a dance."

"Would you dance like that with your brother? No. So you shouldn't with your cousin; no matter how far, it's not right."

"That same night, I went to a blues in Handsworth, and he pulled me again. Only this time, I knew it was him. But when I refused, he grabbed me, and I just gave in to him. And later when he was driving me home. He came off the road and drove straight into Handsworth Park, and that was it. Jesus Christ. He hooked me."

I looked at Henrietta and knew then that the kite rumours had a tail of the truth in them. I recalled how my mother, God mother and Aunty Bertha in responding to the rumours had said:

"If a no so; a soon so. Dem young people don't have no morals."

Nevertheless, they had forgiven her because they had defended her against the church, and even her parents had to forgive her. They defended her by saying that the Rio was a den of iniquity, and pastor had agreed, but he still had her read out of the church because what she had backslid into sin. Aunty Bertha explained that the term 'read out of the church' ended your membership; it was like what the Catholics called excommunication. Those people who followed pastor would not speak to Henrietta, but we were her family, so the rule did not apply to us, so we continued as usual. Then those people excommunicated us because we were blood relatives of a back slider. Next, relatives like Esme's parents, who never spoke to us any way, put out disclaimers that they would not speak to us. I smiled remembering my own experience. She had my sympathy because I too, had my eureka moment the night that of Boy's death and a stranger almost took advantage of me.

"I was rubbed to north coast and back, one night at the Rio." I spoke.

"I know." she replied.

"How?"

"It was the subject of Sunday sermon. The topic was young girls losing their virginity to sinners and back sliders. He all, but mentioned your name, and pastor got the biggest "Amen" we had ever heard in that church."

"Your misfortune was also the subject of his sermon." I spoke.

She nodded. "Pastor spends too much time punishing his congregation, instead of being the good shepherd. Anyway, let me tell you what happened at Charlotte's house before they come."

Charlotte quietly made a pot of tea; we shared a cup and went to the shop on Stony Lane to collect the fish. When we were coming back, we saw Jojo, Salle and Lance going towards Ladypool Road; we stopped and talked for a couple of minutes before heading back to Greet. When we returned to the house the wardrobe was off the landing. There was a peculiar smell of burning coming from the study room, but we thought it was only the scent of ganja. Charlotte made her way up the stairs, and I followed. When she pushed the door of the study room open the smoke gushed into the hallway; a fireball of flame shot past us hitting the opposite wall. We glimpsed Esme lying on the floor, but Geremel had gone. The smell of gas suddenly became overpowering and as we raced to the window, the explosion threw us flying and we landed on the lawn.

We were shocked and relieved at the same time. As we looked up, Esme appeared at the back bedroom with a teddy bear, she pointed at Charlotte, and kept making gestures that seemed to suggest that a child was asleep in the room. Then she put a small face to the window which I was certain was a doll's face. Charlotte ran back into the house screaming. Esme appeared to laugh and beckoned me with her little sixth finger. The fire had fed on the oxygen of Charlotte's screams, and it was as if her fears had increased the carbon of its fierceness, so that the whole house heaved and bellowed like a great, big, monstrous beast. The beckoning sixth finger of Esme and her evil face pressed against the glass where smoke drifted like clouds incensed the once peaceful spirit of the house, which shook animatedly. Its final exhalation was a shower of timber, tumbling plastics, trappings of domestic materials burnt out; fire and smoke began its expiration. The various parts of the house heaved like pods of leviathans, stunned and bewildered; their harpooned bodies with gashing wounds turning the green - white waves of the ocean into red - blue - black waves of blood. The house had become animated, bawling out in its final death throes, and the smoke rose from it like the misty breaths of victims of a medieval plague. I swear I heard a roar.

Chapter Thirty

THREE MONTHS AFTER THE FIRE the remains of. Charlotte, Esme, and Lance interred. The glow of the brightly polished mahogany coffins shone in sharp contrast to the shovelled and obscure dust which they contained. It was a painful sight to see that what we cherished to bury our loved ones in could not facilitate a viewing: a chance to say goodbye; and everyone viewed this as proof of further omens, and unexpected miseries to follow. During the church service, the internment, and the riposte, there were constant nodding of the head by the highly devout; others spoke in tongues; there was weeping, wailing, and gnashing of teeth. The mourners who believed passionately in the Pentecostal, ripped their white shirts and blouses, and threw stones behind their backs while leaving the cemetery, with the words: "Get thee behind me, Satan."

The riposte finished early as it ascended into a church service. Pastor Dingle was in his wasteland, fire, and brimstone mood, and at his insistence in turning the riposte into devotion, people piled out of the Kingston Community Hall, as if they were fleeing the path of a tornado. The moment the food was ready, pastor took over the microphone, and brought on the Handsworth church gospel choir, who sang a beautifully sweet version of "I'll Fly Away." Then in true Pentecostal fervour the second choir sang a rousing version of "When I get to Heaven." All went well until he decided to revisit the internment song, and produced the obituary, and began to whip the diners into redemptive fervour; he off loaded diatribes after diatribes about their sins; he called out to whores, concubines, maids, maidens, whore mongers, apprentice whores, jealous whores and friends, family members burnt with envy; and then he ascended into giving a sermon. People hurriedly ate their refreshments; offered their tables to recently arrived late comers and left; others took their refreshments home as take aways. This tumult became a stampede as people voted with their feet. This rush caused traffic congestion from Soho Road to the fly over at Hockley. It was rumoured that soon after the close relatives had left, someone turned off the public address, and wrestled the microphone from pastor upon his refusal to hand it over. Days after a gloom seemed to hang over the entire ward of Handsworth, which like Brixton, was our Zion, and rock of ages.

Chapter Thirty-One

WHY SINCE THOSE THREE TRAGEDIES, we had become rudderless ships lost at sea? We the young, with new freedoms drifted from church to blues dances; as if realizing our own mortality, suddenly, there were no tomorrows. Cold winters and foggy nights could not stop us going out. There were times when the fog would rise, and we had to wear scarves to cover our mouths and noses. One fore day coming out from the Santa Monica, the fog suddenly descended on Soho Road. It rose like a cloud of salt covering the streets and we had to hold onto buildings that we passed to find our way to Uncle Jeroboam's house on Grange Road. We were lucky to have relatives that lived nearby on Soho Road, or we would have been longer in the fog. Soon we began to love the cold and learned to find our way in the fog. Though we pledged that we would go home every coming summer. How could we as children, run away and go home? How would we travel without passports?

Every year when summer ended, autumn passed us in a flash. With the onset of winter our young bodies yearned for the heat of the sun, and dancing brought us together; as if starved of sunlight, breaking out in hot sweat, and leaving one blues party for another, the cold that cooled us down compensated for an endemic lack of vitamin

D in our growing bones. We had abundant energy, and the boys, raced buses from one stop to the other, just for fun, and we girls, when we walked with straight backs and swaying hips, all men marvelled at our gait, and we controlled our men by making them beg for the merits of our love. We perfected the art form of rub and squeeze. This dance stunned our parents, and again, though disappointed, they accepted it.

The coldness of the weather was turning our hearts to ice, and our emotions to snow. We fought against the elements of the weather that froze our emotions. As the sun brought out the fun and joy of life in the Caribbean, the freezing air of England made our emotions more measured, our decisions more deliberate. The weather of the new country made our responses more manipulative. We were the Windrush generation—though not all of us came by ship—at least a third had travelled by plane. We were taking on the weather, and it was changing us forever. Of all our parents, Uncle Jeroboam was thicker upper lip, colder with his emotions, much more business - like, and controlled everyone.

One afternoon the post man arrived with a telegram for Uncle Jeroboam. He was out the back with my father, whose visits to his house had become more frequent. They were out the back in the garden. Earlier on in the day godmother and Aunty Bertha had arrived to prepare cake samples for Henrietta was finally getting married, or so we thought. I had a feeling something new was up, and I had been lingering, despite Aunt Bernice's instructions that I should look for old recipes in the attic. Mother, godmother, and Aunty Bertha were becoming exasperated with my obstinacy. This refusal was against them, and not aunty Bernice. Henrietta and I had been in the attic before. The three women who were my role models were at times too insistent for me, and I sometimes took immense pleasure in my disobedience. They were in the kitchen, and as usual, I was the cake beater. They were looking for a Bahamas recipe for nutmeg cake but were unsure of the exact ingredients. Grandma Levy was coming up from Bermuda for the wedding, and mother wanted to make Nevis's peppermint patties.

Henrietta arrived with Ismay and Mimi, and Aunty Bertha made the other two girls do the cake beating while we were sent upstairs in the newly renovated attic to search for the missing ingredients for the special treats. Grandma Levy seldom ate these things, but they were special treats for her granddaughter's wedding.

Upstairs in the attic we went going through boxes of books, beside a glass cabinet which contained several copies of the Bible, together with the "Encyclopaedia Britannica." When it came to the "Encyclopaedia Britannica." The oracle at Delphi could not have inspired more confidence; motivated more adherents; received more praise, worshipped more, or accredited with more testimonials of accuracy, than the "Britannica". It was the Septuagint of our missing faith, before the auspicious conversion from the teachings of our father Abraham: a curse which we would soon learn was the result of that misguided act of heresy that has followed our family from its earliest beginnings into the modern age.

Throughout those years insurance agents like carpet baggers had convinced the family and their friends, to twine the sale of this collection of books with insurance policies, which guarded against ignorance and a pauper's grave. It was within those books that I found my forte medicine, and like the Gothic dusk of churches attesting holiness; the saying where there is muck there is money, those dusty boxes attested to the aphorism that where there is dust there is knowledge.

In one of the almost damp cardboard boxes, we came across an exercise book that read "Caribbean Readers' Recipes." Its details coconut cakes, guava cakes, guava jelly cakes and use of plants for ailments and for sex. Henrietta and I laughed. We were wondering when something would give our parents away, and this was it. They were, human beings with desires, despite at times their holiness appeared sanctimonious. We had heard their laughter that brought tears to their eyes when they listened to songs such as "Dr Kitch" and "Big Boy and Teacher," and so many others. And later, our generation will write our very own. We knew the subject of these songs. We knew they made love, and although, they did not shout about it; they did not hide or lie about it either, because we were the results of it. Henrietta cackled and imitated her father's mantra: "Hevry ting in its right proportion Divine; hevry ting." And I laughed, because she could imitate all their voices, as well as the songs.

> "What is dat ting? Big Boy h'ask
>
> "What is dat ting teacher?"
>
> I want to know, Big boy wan know,
>
> What is dat ting?
>
> She said to Big Boy, shut you mouth,
>
> Let me tell you what it's all about .....
>
> She said beli lal be lilal de dush
>
> And reach it you ha fe push...
>
> She said between surround by bush ...

She searched the box. Thumbing through the book we came across both recipes and, prepared to dismount the ladder; but documents that appeared to be official papers caught her eyes, as she closed the box. Hurriedly, she reopened it. They were hand written, and as she turned them over, there were official stamps on every page. There was a birth certificate with a copy of three wills. The birth certificate gave the name of the child as Blades Robertson Dunbar, with Levy, in parenthesis. The place of birth St Johns, Antigua, and the parents' names in the second column as Martha Magdalene Levy, and Joseph Nathaniel Abraham Solomon (Levy) born in St Elizabeth Parish, Jamaica.

"Don't say anything about this. You know what will happen, don't you?"

"We will get licks." I spoke.

Henrietta said, "See, I told you. We are full thorough bred. You remember the last time you got licks it was my mother that beat you."

"What was that about?" I inquired.

"I don't remember exactly, but when you got home, you got some more from Uncle Blades, remember?"

"That is long ago. How do you expect me to remember that?"

"You would forget because the next time you stayed with us, you were so nice: it was ""yes, taunty Divine, and no taunty Divine; and I love you, taunty Divine."" "And she had made you the nice dress that you came to be measured for in the first place and you wouldn't let her touch you; it was so pretty, I almost felt jealous."

"I remember now; it was for Rudy's wedding."

"She got aunty Marva on the phone, and she was nearly in tears, saying her niece thinks she is a molester". ""Kuya, Miss Woman tink me have time to waste. De gull a gwan bad, lek me his ha molesta.""

""Bang her arse, damn feisty, likkle gal pickney."" "Aunty Marva had said, and you got three a de best. Is good thing you was wearing a slip."

We thought we heard footsteps below and became silent. After they had gone, she said:

"I remember, we only got beat when we had slips on."

"See how clever they are?" I replied.

"And the boys had to wear merino."

"They not stupid." she said.

We laughed. Then exclaimed:

"See if we let out that we know their secret, there will be big trouble; they will say ""we send you for this, and you come back with that. That is carry go, bring come. Interfering in our own business.""

"You know, I don't like trouble."

"That's our secret. Cross my heart and hope to die; to be your best friend on resurrection morning. Promise to be bury you if I don't die first."

"Amen." I said, and we descended the ladder and the stairs like two angels coming down from heaven.

But when we came down there was trouble. There was a strong family gathering, because even Rudy was there. Uncle Jeroboam had more than one concern. The government in Grand Cayman wanted clarification regarding the preferred nationality of owners of the Levy Estate, and there were complications for Santiago, in both Grand

Cayman and Australia regarding his status. What was nearer the bone, however, concerned the latest conduct of Santiago.

The brother of Josiah Mandelbaum, Dunbar Levy, like Uncle Dada, had brown hair, fair skin; loved women and women loved him. He died at the age of thirty—three eaten by sea crocodiles that swam the one hundred and sixty-three miles between Cuba and Jamaica's north coast.

Before he died, however, he had set up shops, businesses and built seven homes in Santiago de Cuba, where he had fathered seven children by three local women. Santiago Dunbar Levy was his youngest son, because true to the revolutionary spirit of Jamaica, six of his seven sons had volunteered under Che, and they had been killed fighting in the Cuban revolution.

Santiago was the sole survivor and therefore, in his will. Like his father before him he too loved danger and with us all, temptation is a strong Levy trait. Being obsessively head strong, he had wasted no time in striking up a love affair with Linda, despite he knew she was his cousin's estranged wife.

The love affair between the two passionate relatives had hit the streets of Kingston, long before the telegram had arrived. The happy, loving couple had gone to Grand Cayman where they stayed for a short while looking after the estate which grew copra. They attended parties at Mona, and Hanover Street, and enjoyed ska dances. Santiago had begun to spend time between Grand Cayman and Mandeville, overseeing the pimento crops. Uncle Dada thought they had settled in the Caribbean, but suddenly they were back in Victoria. He had asked Uncle Jeroboam what course of action to take. At the same time, he had advised him to disinherit Santiago, and evict them from his house, or find alternative accommodation for the loving couple. The most vocal suggestion that he should return to Mandeville did not appeal to his thirst for exile, and an impasse had developed between Uncle Dada, and Uncle Jeroboam.

While this disagreement continued, Henrietta and I looked at each other, and winked, remembering the documents that we had just discovered in the attic. The discussion continued.

Uncle Jeroboam had warned uncle Dada that if such outrage ever happened, then it would be Uncle Dada' s responsibility to resolve. After all, he argued the misalliance had taken place under his roof. Yet, like two beasts they had locked horns, and responsibility kept shifting back and forth from Australia to England, and from England, back to Australia.

The argument from Uncle Dada's point of view rested on the irrefutable premise that Uncle Jeroboam was Rudy's father. He held the view that Linda was the mother of Uncle Jeroboam's grandchildren, and that made her behaviour Uncle Jeroboam's responsibility.

Whereas Uncle Jeroboam argued that since he was his elder by five years, the conduct having taken place under his roof, the facts were more than obvious that as executor of Dunbar Levy's will, the act of impropriety had taken place under his watch, with double responsibility over the heir of the decease, and he was dictating a letter to Ishish, as response to Uncle Dada's surrealistic resistance.

After that letter, three weeks had passed, and the dust seemed to have settled the matter, until the seventh week, when Uncle Jeroboam was in receipt of yet another telegram from Uncle Dada. It reported the premature death of Santiago and requested funds from his father's estate. He knew his family well enough, and aware that Australia was too far from a distance for anyone to attend the funeral, had quickly cremated the body. Although the telegram ended in sombre tones, the act of cremation was against the teachings of our father Abraham, and the entire family descended, initially, into despair, followed by hurricanes of arguments, fierce disputes and ended with lamentations. The church once again cited the burning of the dearly departed as further proof of the curse of the Levy and Solomon pool of incest and bigotry.

The short life of Santiago encapsulates in a coconut, the consequences which we all must face for decisions that we have made in our lives. But there are undercurrents to whom we might think we are, and these run-like ghosts embedded in linchpins of our genes. Santiago had swam the one hundred and sixty-three miles between Ochi Rios and Santiago de Cuba seven times. Like his father before him he began swimming by making his own harpoons. The harpoons were made by straightening and filing wires that came from the sugar factory. These wires bounded the chaff that came from the sugar cane stalks when the dry stalks were returned to the siding from the sugar factory. Santiago fashioned the fish - gun by using recycled pieces of pine wood. He made grooves in the body of the fish - gun from where the short spears would release when he hunted fish at the bottom of the sea. The trigger operated a lever that released each spear. He cut strips of rubber from a bicycle tube and placed them either side of the wood. They gave tension. As was the custom, his goggles further adaptations of the bicycle tube. He had rounded a piece of glass and fixed it into this frame. His swimming shorts and vest of rubber kept him warm in the colder parts of his dives. Santiago wore his gear with such pride. He was stylish, such a magnificent sight that the locals and tourists took snaps of him when he strolled out of the sea, body beautiful.

In his home-made gear he would go out alone, the sole solitary diver taking on the waves; he learnt to swim using one leg, and one arm so that he could rest the other leg and arm for when he got tired. Like other fish divers of the Caribbean, he joined the breed apart and, developed lungs like tadpoles. A strong swimmer, he could float as well. The fishing was good business, but he craved a more stretched and challenging relationship with the sea. He wanted to be a world beater and where else, but in his own back yard? He had conquered the two hundred odd miles between Montego Bay and Santiago de Cuba in six hours; the three hundred odd miles between Grand Cayman and Santiago de Cuba in seven and a half hours, and from his experience in Australia he wanted to take a speed boat home to extend his swim challenges, as well as develop speed boat racing.

The morning of the twenty fifth of April was unlike any other day. The day seemed washed with white light. At the Victoria Speed Boat Club, Santiago, Linda, and Mary, were strapped in their seats for the ride of a lifetime. The boat looked dashing with the Jamaican flag painted across the hull, and its occupants in their Trinidad calypso shirts. They cut a good style, as they set off, along the coast. Santiago had heard of the Twelve Apostles, and true to his religious nature had been fascinated by the stones in the sea that bore the name of biblical characters; he wanted to give each one an individual name.

They set off slowly, picking their way along the coast. The network of small towns seemed grouped under the same name, because, although, each seemed different when they had passed through by road, as the speed of the boat picked up and they receded into the background, looking back they all looked like one town: the same. Dotted along the coastline they reminded Santiago of the discovery cities of Panama, Costa Rica, and, especially, Cuba, where the land like a forced woman, submissively, surrendered her body, even more to deny her heart to the new, and unworthy captors.

Travelling west to east from Portland, Discovery Bay passed in a blur, locked in a moment.

At the wheel, he looked askance at the Great Ocean Road that seemed an endless and extended thread with a dawn of stitches. If he had time, he would have closed his eyes, when Linda rested her head on his shoulder, and imagined that they were somewhere in the western Caribbean. The sea spread like a sheet of blue satin, and the Southern Ocean sky, arched from the horizon over the sea to the land, bright as a cathedral' s dome of glass. Opaque as the cathedrals of stone so grieved by the broken black people of Australasia. Uncanny, how, sometimes the Southern Ocean felt like home.

Past Point Fairy, they were at the Shipwreck Coast at last. Santiago raced past place names that Telford had told him about that lay within the one hundred and ten miles or so distance to the place named for a Greek and Roman God; only that countless paean had been sung at the Apostles before, when Arrente had carved his cathedrals of stone, and the rugged coastline that swept before him. Then he saw the pillars of limestone, rising columns ascending out of the sea, broken, but counted twelve to signifying the absent four as counted dead, or already taken up into heaven by rapture.

He switched the engine off and let the craft drift for a while, while they ate lunch. Thirty minutes or so must have passed because they could not see the Great Ocean Road anymore. The Apostles seemed ever so far away. They had drifted pass Brisbane, and he knew he had saved enough fuel to get back, but they were off course, farther out than he had bargained for, or as the coast guards had advised. He turned the craft around and headed back to Portland.

The spirit of the alligator within him must have fought with the crocodile for like his father at sea, both hunted his heart.

The sea which was calm before suddenly turned; it took on a rough, greenish white foam that lashed against both sides of the boat; the wind began to howl like a sick and rabid dog about their ears, and as he steered the craft past Gibson Steps, he could see the brown sand, now that the view was on his best side. He shouted to Linda to put the life jacket on, but he ought to have done this earlier; ought not to have taken them off to have lunch; ought to have replaced them immediately after they had eaten, no matter how calm the sea. The waves and something in the waves wanted him and had been tracking him all along.

At Loch Ard Gorge, the boat banked, then, swerved. There was the sound of a great thud, as it hit an object like the head of an enormous rock in the water. This caused it to lift into the air. Then it tumbled back, overturning - swirling like a coin tossed into a fountain it plunged beneath the blue—black waves. A maelstrom rose where it had re-entered the sea, and a great cry, an inhuman cry

- a mighty cry resounding like an angry verb that gave immediate and violent gratification, rang through the air, and waters of the bay churned and lifted into hilltop waves threatening the shore and the Great Ocean Road. Yet, clinical in its wake, the Southern Ocean pulled back, and rushed the tiny craft, and the wind delivered death, straight to the heart.

Chapter Thirty-Two

U NCLE DADA'S CELEBRITY STATUS HAD been won on the battlefield; then jostling with fellow soldiers in the hierarchy of men and, in maintaining his prominence in the face of barbarians who would deny his humanity. Uncle Dada did not suffer fools long. He had flown from Australia and stayed overnight in London before travelling to Birmingham.

Rudy and Jimmy Mackintosh went to collect him and his family at Elmdon Airport. They had, as most people do, when picking up friends or relatives whom they have not seen for a long time. They wrote his name on a placard and were holding this up at the arrivals' entrance. They thought it was one of those days when arrivals were slow and thought nothing out of the ordinary had happened. Therefore, they continued to wait patiently. Three hours later they were still waiting and went to the desk to make inquiries.

They gave his name; description, and general protected characteristics, but there was no help. The officials seemed overwhelmed and confused. Meanwhile, Rudy and Jimmy were getting heated, because the officials kept asking the same questions to which they had already given the answers. They waited while they inquiries were made to find out whether he had boarded the internal fight from London to Birmingham.

As they were about to give up waiting, an official rushed forward and asked them to a nearby office. They were taken to the office, and there were three the policemen. The inner door to the office opened and Uncle Dada appeared with his young wife and child; he seemed more annoyed than distraught. The officer in charged was explaining to him that he had not received permission from the Australian government to travel with his wife and child outside country as they were both wards of the country. Then they explained the situation to Rudy and Jimmy:

"Your uncle was stopped, behind customs because he needed to show that he has documentary proof for the woman and child." the female custom's officer informed.

"This is an internal flight." Rudy intoned. "Are you stupith?"

The officer ignored Rudy and addressed Uncle Dada." Are you sure you haven't any papers at all; we have contacted Australia House, and they are adamant that travelling papers were issued for the woman and child?"

"Perhaps, you have misplaced them, or left them in your hotel room in London, sir." said another.

They kept up a friendly enough talk with Uncle Dada, but all they received was a stony silence. His wife Dell kept looking at him amused, by their insistence. The three-year-old child clung to her father, and stared at her new relatives, fixing them with a steady look, the way that curious fascination that children have for fresh faces.

The officers were becoming frustrated, and turned to Uncle Dada's two British relations:

"I understand they will be staying with you, here in Birmingham." said one of the officers.

Neither Rudy nor Jimmy volunteered an answer.

"Yes. We staying wid them." Della answered.

The officers smiled, pleased that at last they were they were getting somewhere.

"Yes, Mrs Levy, and a pleasant stay in Birmingham, to you."

"Thank you." Della answered.

They turned to Uncle Dada. "We are sorry for the hold up, the inconvenience. We understand that you were in the war, and now live down under. It is a pleasure to meet you, sir." This was met with a stony silence, until Della pushed her husband to answer. She beamed with glee, and touched his arm, and Uncle Dada, said:

"Yes; yes. Yes, thank you." But that was all.

When they arrived from the airport, we were all overjoyed to see little Martha Levy, Della, and, of course, Uncle Dada. Popular though he was, they were the stars of the show. There were competitions to decide where they would stay. In the end the family decided that they would stay in Handsworth for the first week; Sutton Coldfield the next, and Waterston for the third week. They had come for a month, and the final week would be their decision.

Three days after I arrived from choir practice in the evening. Usually, I would shout that I was home, bound up the stairs, place my Bible on the dresser; say my prayers, thanking God for an honest family, mostly with good hearts; run a hot shower and drift to island shores in my mind. Then look at my college work, phone around; waited for supper, and bound downstairs. It was a regular routine with me.

When I put my key in the outer door, it opened as usual, but not the porch door. That was unusual that I should have to ring the bell. Mother came to the door, much better dressed than usual, and ushered me before this pale skin woman, whose picture was on the wall, surrounded by people of assorted complexions.

She was seated left of the fireplace, near the window and must have seen me walk to the door. She was not scary but looked as if she might be if you did not know how to approach her. I let myself be dragged before her as she sat rocking back and forth in the rocking chair that Uncle Jeroboam would never allow anyone to sit in when it was at his house. He had brought it to Sutton Coldfield the week before, and I wondered if they would take this chair from place to place whilst she was there so that it followed her around.

"Cherry Blossom." Mother said, as though I had been brought before a Queen.

Benign, a smile that scrambled your brain, and tugged at your heart strings, she looked me straight in the eye as if I ought to know her name; her position; her mission.

"Good evening, Nana!" I said, and curtsied.

How was I to know that it was expected? There was some talk about women of her generation in the Caribbean being hereditary god daughters of Queen Victoria, so I suppose it was the right thing to do. After all, the portrait of Queen Vicki had pride of place, among the pictures that had been framed and displayed on the living room wall. I must have done the right thing, because she got up out of her seat, slowly, helped by mother, who jumped to her aid, and embraced me. It was the sweetest embrace, I have ever had, and she broke my heart, but in a wonderful way.

Then she sat down, and I was dumb founded, as if this woman had heard everything about me, and I now had to be careful, because to be in her presence was like being in the presence of Queen Vicki, as she was her representative, and God's representative on earth. She was cause of the box upstairs with so many papers; she oversaw all the houses we had; all the money we had, and when she passed, she would have all these people fighting to carry her cortege, because she was the Mater.

Any moment now, I expected the others to invade your house; invade your room; take over your space and take over the place. Then as warning of the shape of things to come, there was the commotion. It was as if Uncle Dada had rounded up the whole of Handsworth and had brought them to our door. A small group of men and women came up to the porch, and he marched them in, shouting his aunt's name and laughing. The others were in conversations.

He had loud and jovial friends, and was even so himself and, shouted for Uncle Jeroboam, and everyone came to greet him. But as he came before Nana, there was an air of solemnity. His entourage melted away, mingling with the rest of the house, and were received by the family, and friends that were already there.

Uncle Dada, his wife Dell, and little Martha each kissed Nana, singly and knelt at her feet. Nana beamed with delight. Then he bid his wife and child to hold hands and form a group of three kneeling around Nana's rocking chair, and had their picture taken. The flash of the camera they had brought from Australia, flashed brightly, with tinsel magic.

Family and friends of the family came in droves. In fact, it was a mark of disrespect not to come unannounced. So, I braced myself for more invasions, and knew that we would have complaints from the neighbours, who because of all the cars, the sheer glee, the bliss, the delight would not be able to differentiate a family conference or a funeral from a blues party. I knew that in the end Uncle Jeroboam would say:

> "Dem faas; them too damn faaas …fish outa water, we do
> not belong ya."

And all the aunts and uncles would agree. Then at school when we spoke about the gathering, the native children would say.

"That sounded great; could we come next time?"

And we would say, our hearts still throbbing with glee:

"Course ya can."

Jay and his friends always came. And it was great. We like it when the children of God, troop the colours.

They had baked her treats: the Nevis peppermint patties, sweet not savoury; the Jamaica rum cake; the Bahamas nutmeg. I cut her three slices; three because mother had shown me how to cut them paper thin, because she could not eat things that were too sweet. And I served them on a tray. When I brought the cake in, I saw she had four beautiful rings on her fingers. They were bespoke, made of Guyanese and Honduras gold, with Surinam diamonds, and I was so surprised I kept staring at both her hands and the beautiful rings on her fingers. She must have known but pretended not to notice my fascination.

"Bring my Bible from upstairs." she said."

As I was about to go upstairs, I heard the key turn in the door and Henrietta came in all flushed and flustered. I should have known someone had been walking up to the door when Nana was peeking through the lace curtain. Mother brought her before Nana, and she too, curtsied.

"Good evening, Nana?" she said, and knelt at the chair.

Nana laughed and fondled her hair. "Ya 'ave hair like mine. Get up chile."

Henrietta rose and sat on the sofa. Mother gave her a little plate with cake; she took it, then thanked her, and sat looking at Nana, every now and then. Instead of making my way upstairs, I sat beside Henrietta and leaned back into the sofa. Like her, I was equally fascinated by the ancient and could not hide my curiosity. Nana was equally fascinated by us, but accepted our occasional stares, and maintained a calm, and quiet dignity. She was accustomed to being in control of situations and accepted our wonderment.

In the next hours that passed the house began to fill with people. The grand invasion had begun, and there was a grand surprise as well. After so many years pastor Dingle visited our home. He came with godfather Natty, Aunty Bertha and godmother Sweetie. It was so unusual seeing Aunty Bertha without King Jaja, that I almost asked for him. But I stopped myself just in time by putting my hand to my mouth. Rudy brought the boys: Joseph, Jay, Lance, Salle, and Laban. And people continued to come. They poured into the house: kneeling at Nana's rocking chair; curtsying; and she was in her element with kisses from everyone.

It was as if the Anancy stories that Aunty Bertha had told us how the four brothers of Nanny had come to her town to pledge their allegiance, had come alive. I winked, and kept on winking throughout the evening, as one by one people came to curtsy, as I did, or knelt beside her rocking chair; and I marvelled how graciously she had received everyone and counted how many kisses she gave and how many she had received. For all of us it was clear that she had been blessed by God: he had given her four score years and ten; and one extra year more for grace, to pass her wisdom to the next generation, and keep alive in our memories the legacy of her uncle Qao, to pass on the twin torches of her legacy to her descendants and set us aright.

She wanted to be anointed on such an occasion, not even Uncle Jerome, who was at loggerhead with his family could be absent, without it being a mark of great disrespect. At first it was a little awkward when he turned up, but my father went to the door and hugged him; and when he seemed to linger at the doorway, he pulled him into the porch. Uncle Jerome allowed himself to be dragged into the house.

Then Uncle Jeroboam came from the dining room and kissed him on the cheek and they both began to cry. Uncle Charlie, who was Esme's godfather had only seen his brother at the funeral when his daughter and God daughter were buried, because of him being Charlotte's father was also ready to forgive. They all stood in the porch, blocking people coming in and aunty Marva came and said:

"Genklemen. Genklemen. Genklemen! We all know it is an auspicious h'occasion. But wid due respects, G- e-n-k-l-e-m-e-n. Please may we 'ave dis door?"

Everybody began to laugh, as the four came inside and Uncle Jerome went straight to the living room and knelt at the feet of Martha. And she played with his ear and said: "Kuya; someone just touched me 'eart. Thank you, Lord." And everyone clapped; and he rose and went to the kitchen to embrace Aunty Bertha, and they kissed.

Then pastor Dingle took over our house with a long everlasting prayer; so long that I shall not even attempt to write it. All I shall say is he reminded us of our past errors and insisted that they must be things of the past; sins; transgressions now behind us, and the need for consecration. All admonitions before he came to the main event.

"Han now. De main gatherin here. This anointing. In the name of our Lord and Saviour Jesus de Christ. De ongly begotten Son of God. Behols what manner of man. Dat 'e should leave 'is 'ome on 'igh to vacant 'is throne of gold to walk 'is feet h'on bitta h'earth; to dwell in the cold, cold universe to cleave de worrld fer all h'our sins. Amen."

That must have been a signal, to follow suit. Everybody said: "Amen."

Then Deacon Windrush - so named because he was born on the ship coming up from Jamaica - came with the cloth of purity and placed it about the neck of Nana, and pastor Dingle said.

"Who has the Bible?"

It was then that I remembered it was the first thing that she had told me to do. Luckily there was one on the table in the hallway, which I hurriedly gave to pastor Dingle.

"And what is the text?" he asked.

"Bereishith twenty … chapter twenty h'eight; verse two." said Nana.

Deacon Windrush turned to the chapter, and read:

"Arise, go to Padanaram, to the house of Bethuel thy mother's father; and take thee a wife from thence of the daughters of Laban thy mother's brother."

"Who 'as de wine?" said pastor Dingle.

"I 'as de wine." Aunty Bertha responded.

Pastor Dingle took the wine; sprinkled a little on the floor.

Then handed the glass to Nana. She took the glass and drank.

"What is the second text?" He inquired, a second time.

Nana looked at him and said: "Do not be yoked with the unrighteous like oxen to the plough, for when the one head turns right; the other shall go left; and like the good and the bad, when linked together, one with nothing shall gain an evil doer, but the good shall lose their soul, h'an perish."

"That is not in our scripture." said pastor Dingle.

"Well, it is the second Corinthians Chapter six; verse fourteen." Deacon Windrush informed. Thumbing through the Bible, he read:

"Do not be yoked together with unbelievers. For what does righteousness and wickedness have in common, or what friendship can goodness have of badness?"

Then he broke the newly baked unleavened bread, which she took and placed it on her tongue.

Then he took the oil of olives from the place called Gethsemane, among the groves of vines where Naboth had planted his vineyard;

poured it into the cup of redemption, and anointed her head, and as he did so, he repeated these words:

"Martha Magdalene Solomon Levy, I anoint you in the name of God: the father Almighty; the Son, and the Holy Spirit of redemption, and consecrate this act of devotion into whose hands I through the love of God, believing in the resurrection, entrusts into the arms of the Almighty. Amen."

We watched as Nana received the anointing with grace and humility, and all assembled, voiced in one accord: "Amen."

But he continued. "Thou anointed my head with oil, my cup of redemption running over. For sure, goodness and mercy shall fill my cup, all the days of my life, I dwell in the house of God forever, and forever. Amen."

Meanwhile this had been going on Henrietta and Laban had sneaked into the kitchen, and were helping with the plates, and the rest of the dishes. This was unusual, for Laban was not the kind of male to volunteer assistance in any kitchen. At first, I thought nothing of it, and I do not think anyone else had taken any notice the way that they were flirting with each other. But I caught the look in their eyes as they brought the rest of the dishes into the living room, which had been turned into the third dining room for the occasion.

'Now the dispensation of 'Devarim', the first book of the Tanakh and the fifth book of Torah. For sayeth Elohim. I shall raise you up above the fallen and the wicked nations. But before, curses shall come upon you. The seed of your loving shall scatterer forever. Until you accept the glory bestowed upon you from the beginning.'

These big words were always a feature of his sermons and were the hall marks of his fame. It was the enormous pride of his congregation whenever he used Hebrew and Latin words, which for many were signs that their pastor was blessed and truly a man ordained by God, because he spoke the languages of God.

'Amen!' the whole housed, even those in the dining room and the kitchen chorused.

And he anointed Nana a second time with Olive oil.

The only persons that were not paying close attention was Esme and Laban. They were laughing and giggling until Uncle Jeroboam was called into the kitchen to scold them. He did so and left it at that. As far as we were all concerned there had been enough trouble between Uncle Jerome's children and the rest of the family, and we were all looking forward to re-establishing the loving relationship that we had enjoyed before the rift. I saw what the outcome of their singling out each other might become, and grew afraid what the future might hold, but realized that I could not say much. After all, she might have been chosen for Laban, and her proposed outside marriage would be "unequally" yoked, because her lover had refused conversion.

In the meantime, however, Iron Sound was around the back; the huge speaker boxes had been hitched up and the music strayed throughout the house, the back yard and into the outhouse. There was dancing in the outhouse, too, and Henrietta and Laban seemed to have teamed up because the house itself was for the adults, while the young people entertained themselves away from their parents in the outhouse round the back. The lights were out and there was dancing in the middle of the floor and in the dark and cosy corners. This was done because friends; the friends of friends, and relatives were there. But you were not expected to dance with relatives like that in the dark jamboree corner, where people took the chance to hook someone. I was hooked before, and decided not to go there, so I just danced with my girl cousins and refused to dance with any males, whether they were relatives or not, because being hooked made your body yearn for love. And heaven was declared; dancers broke loose when the DJs played "In the Midnight Hour".

I had ear worms for my favourite songs. But a special infection for the main song that I loved the most. There was music the like of which I had never heard before, and many songs that we had heard before. It was a beautiful occasion, and we heard so much music that your ears began to ring like bells, your heart throbbed and the vibrations from the boxes shook your whole body. There was great laughter and whistles and shouts of joy from the house itself. We learned later that the noise was because Nana had got up and danced. And like me her favourite song was "In the Midnight Hour."

Chapter Thirty-Three

THREE MONTHS DOWN THE LINE - the season being winter - the charred, four walls of the house looked like the charcoal remains of a mammoth roasted slowly and deliberately in a crater of fire polka - dotted with flakes of snow.

Within its walls, in its damp, dank, dark recesses, I roamed, still haunted by the flash of light, the spectre of my own body as a walking ball of fire, and painful searing of my own burning flesh. Death by fire is like the melting of a burning candle, its self - consuming flame eating away the fat dripping down, from tip to stem, feeding the devouring combustion igniting it, in the first place; and God has promised the descendants of Noah, not judgement by water, but purification by fire in the next world to come. In the next Armageddon, the fire next time!

The soul imperishable as a flash of fire, I looked for a shell to house my soul, and found it in the Anancy tale of the turtle, who must carry its house forever on its back, with its head for a helmet, that once rode the back of a crocodile.

The crocodile said: "I know you can swim; you live on land as well as water; you cannot drown. Give me a good reason why I should carry you to the other side of the river."

"It is because I cannot drown, and God will repay you with wisdom." the turtle replied.

"What good is wisdom? Can't you see I' m a crocodile?"

"Wisdom is the beginning of all that is good. It is a talent from the very dawn of creation."

"I do not need it. Here in the water, it is foolish to be wise."

"But if you have the skills to persuade your fellow beings, and have them do as you say, there's wisdom for you."

"Look", said the crocodile, becoming agitated. "I am here at the water's edge, waiting to rescue a talented monkey from the jaws of a shark, or the mouths of alligators, and you come here with politics and argument?"

"It is my job to see the world is fair and good for everyone."

"What's in it for me then?" the crocodile intoned.

"God will bless and keep you safe from the hunters who come to this pool every day to kill and hunt your kind." said the turtle.

"I see them come: all humans, some with spears; others with sticks of fire." replied the crocodile.

"Now here is my first piece of wisdom. They need your young eggs for food to eat; your tail for whips of fire; your tongue to talk to God; your skin for shoes and handbags, your bones for museums, and your flesh as a delicacy. They say it provides traction for their second favourite past time."

"What's that?" asked the crocodile.

"They clone themselves." the turtle replied.

"Well, what's the good in that?"

"They're envious of our kind… so many eggs."

The crocodile grew silent; creased its brows; opened its eyes, flexed its jaws, and yawned.

"That was funny… so many eggs. I like that; funny."

They both laughed. Then the turtle said, "They also believe your tongue is a letter from God that tells of the end of the world, and what will happen in the next creation story."

"Man is made of dust." replied the crocodile.

"No; he is not. Man is water. Ask the monkey. There is another piece of wisdom I have given you." said the turtle.

The crocodile began to cry, though, not to the surprise of the turtle.

"What's wrong?" asked the turtle.

"I see where you bury your eggs, and when you go across the river, I fully intended to dig them up and feed them to my young for food." she said

"I know that, but leave one of the hatches, so that a soul might be saved; a soul that is repentant and in need of a newly washed, contrite heart. Let's say a new contract of redemption. Let even one of that live, and I will forgive you the worse evil."

"You take risks." said the crocodile.

"I risk everything." the turtle said and prepared to swim to the other side of the river.

Three days later, she spotted the crocodile basking in the sun on the opposite shore and shouted across the river: "I still have my heart!"

"I knew you wouldn't have given it way!" replied the crocodile.

The fourth voice: I am the spirit of the turtle, slow to anger, but wise. Having lived a life of contradictions, I have washed my soul in the rivers of redemption, but I have a new spirit that seeks a shell and have found a tent of skin in my cousin Henrietta.

The day I possessed her, that night I danced, my entire body tingling with life. Having possessed a living being and attracted the attention of a lover, I wandered the dance hall that night with such allure, that even if Laban had any doubt about committing himself to the spell, it would have been impossible, futile, anyway.

A restless and furtive spirit I would try to speak to my friends and family, but no one would see me; I even tried to join in their conversations, but no one would hear me. Once I walked in front of my own father, but he ignored me, as he did in real life. Indeed, you might say I have no right to be lonely because I have Charlotte and Ismay with me, but the moment we reached Nadarina, they held hands and disappeared. I have since chased Laban at night when he is walking alone, or sleeping, so that I might have a companion, a friend, and a lover of my own. I need centripetal force to experience love that will make me feel like I am alive like a woman again. Every time my song played, I was alive again, dancing among the throngs in the midnight hour.

The months following, the fog rose, and I tried to escape the Alpine weather, for more clement, warmer climes. I roamed the cemetery looking for a route to escape, but there was none. After shock I looked for an abiding place but found none to my satisfaction. The soul being like a bird, I took flight, and though, perplexed, I followed a flock of flamingos to find a southern sky, but only my mind had grown wings.

Upon my return to England, I frequented the museums of the dead; looked at the fear and admiration of the living as they marvelled at the dishevelled mummies of the dead. From there I joined libraries and read about the horrors of the blood thirsting and avenging lioness Sekhmet that devoured their bodies and ate the souls of men; I read about Kali with twelve arms that collected the skulls of her enemies; shrunk their heads into tiny beads and wore them on necklaces, or just simply used them as materials to enhance the architecture of her many palaces. Reader, I committed evil and dastardly deeds.

Chapter Thirty-Four

T HE HARD TIMES PROVED ME right. I had been right all along. It is an evil world. It struck me that the world in which we lived was a terrible, terrible place, where brutality, hatred and the might of power were the only way to exist, and the devil was firmly in control. The merits of existence then became the ability to commit to evil. In my case.

It happened in one of my past lives or on one of my trips to the neighbouring towns of Birmingham when we visited churches for concerts, fellowship, and sometimes as young people, just out of curiosity and a sense of nothing better to occupy our time. It happened on a foggy and misty afternoon in Redditch when I was walking down the hill. I saw them coming towards me in the mist. Even before they reached me the temperature had dropped. The wind soared, but although gently, there was a sudden chill.

They came towards me bursting out of a cloud of fog, and I trembled; there was a tremor in the air too. They wore black, which contrasted so well with the dry whiteness all around because there was no snow on the ground; there was only fog. And as they passed, he outside of her and her almost brushing my shoulders, he at first seemed oblivious of me, until we passed. He looked askance at me and hissed. Then placing his arm around her shoulder, as if shielding her away from me he said: "Be mindful Cathy." Her face lit up and a smile creased her face; her face held a deathly paleness; yet pale and placid as she looked, her countenance emitted a kind beauty, like the poetic licence of a verse of pure and petulant poetry. It all happened so quickly as we passed, and when I looked back, they had gone, vanished into the fog of reality, and enveloped in the foggy reaches of time. The look of evil had beguiled my soul. The beauty of her face, at once beautiful was also evil and impure while his face was white as a sheet, in one sense arrogant, evil, but in another, handsome, beautiful, and pure. This same might had struck my great ancestor as one of the many infants that they locked in the storeroom coming from the Bight of Benin.

They had searched me out; selected me and by silent pact had chosen me to consummate their marriage of good and evil. I had the stigmata of whips carved on the ploughed flesh of my back and cries I had heard and whippings that I had endured that I carried welts on my back, too, and scar tissues within my scarred, scared, and embattled soul. The decision to which I had arrived placed me in a position in which I would haunt and torment the lives of the descendants of the capitalists who had sold and bartered my ancestors, turning them into items and articles of exchange. Since immersing myself in their marriage of evil and good, since that is the way, they viewed the world.

Chapter Thirty-Five

I T WAS NOT LONG BEFORE I found the meaning of this persistent dream that had haunted me for as long as I could remember as a child. Lying on my back or in a foetal position. I would let my mind drift into two places that were quite opposite but equally frightening. One was a river which was calm and peaceful. Yet, this came at a price. It was one of the places where the dead were thrown into holes in the ground, without ceremony, without pathos.

The other place sat beside a stony stream in a desert filled with crocodiles. It was a terrain interspersed with beauty and fear that made it a place of contradictions. Its fearsome beauty seemed filled with vile ugliness, and I would jolt myself whenever my mind was drifting into this place. Then pinch my arm to stay awake. Yet, both places seemed not to exist one without the other. They were the beauty and the beast of my existence, and their contrasts filled my dreams with vengeance and gave shine and sparkle to my imagination.

Since then, my cause was vengeful I learned quickly how to gain the trust of the families. I hired myself out as a domestic worker and became a travelling evangelist. This was a familiar role, and with its implicit superior and subordinate roles it was part of the traditional master, mistress slave relationship upon which capitalism was built. And religion is a medium of passion and faith for people who communicate well. The first families to hire me were the Cob family that lived in Liverpool; the Barclay and Lloyd families of London, Birmingham, and Bristol.

It was a dull winter's day in nineteen sixty - seven. The train limped into Bristol Temple Mead Station. They met me at the station and took me home to show me off like children who had been bought a brand, new toy. At first, they treated me well, but somehow it did not take long before they showed the customary contempt and ingratitude. I then began to use my powers against them in their homes and at the parties they threw. I began to target their guests by scaring them at nights that made them crash their cars. I had become a mhondoro yemudzimu – a guardian lion ancestral spirit but sometimes I transformed into Kali. On one occasion I even turned into Sekhmet the devouring lioness and ate humans.

Once upon a time when the moon was bright in a charcoal night, and I worked as a servant in the one of the better suburbs of the city of Bristol. When I arrived at that city, on the south side, two demons had possessed a tax collector who lived near the cemetery at Brockhall. We met at the corner of the street, near Brockhall End. The family claimed that seven spirits had possessed him for seven years, and could I exorcise all seven of the spirits. The spirits were not violent, but they were surprised when I called each of the demons by name, as the one gave chase to the other, as one - by – one, he became cleansed of their impurities.

Standing there, I was about to place them in the s stray dogs and feral cats that roamed the streets, but they pleaded with me to be placed in pigeons, they said, because they might redeem themselves from the boredom of evil. I turned and cornered them in the alley and, they cried aloud:

'We are the sins of our fathers but spare the possessed who are not responsible for the sins of their fathers.'

But it was my resolve to avenge the atrocities of the fathers. Still, a voice within me said: 'You have come to this place to avenge the dead; to eat the hearts of their descendants and rid them of their souls.'

But all the devils were babbling, so I ran from that place and left the evangelists terror – stricken but returned to the church and set the seven pigeons to peck out the eyes of all believers in idolatry. I continued my merciless onslaught upon all the descendants of those demons who had bewitched my fathers in Chatterley.

Chapter Thirty-Six

Lost in whirlwinds I travelled to distant lands but found no abiding place. Then one day, a family of six came to the cemetery, where I was seated on a bench that had been dedicated to a kindly soul, and out of respect I sat there, a far off, so as not to interrupt the internment and engaging a living soul in conversation, they showed me kindness, and I followed their footprints out of the cemetery; got into a car, and ended up outside the house where my grandmother Martha had come to visit.

Like all her descendants I knelt at her feet, and she was the only one that could see me, because she too was about to die. She blessed me with kisses, as she did all the others; there being no favourite among us. And later that night I possessed Henrietta, as she danced in the dark, and cavernous corner, where the music was sweetest, and where I knew love unabated would thrive and blossom. That was the mote.

That was the way we danced, two bodies locked together in rhythm, defying gravity, and I danced and danced and danced. In the past life I had danced like this to so many songs, and we had so many favourite tunes from a time when the cerebral world we inhabited was always segregated from the rest and the songs were for us to express the joys of music. From Shirley Lewis' "Hello Stranger;" Etta James' "Twenty-Four Hours; "or her "I'd rather Go Blind," to Barbara Masons' "Yes, I'm Ready." The men never held us back because on the dance floor women ruled; in the home: in the kitchen we ruled, in the bedroom we had to be satisfied; with checks and balances, we were equals in a black and segregated world.

I danced in the body of my cousin, until she was exhausted, and still I would not let her go. Not until I heard someone call my name: "Esme must be here. I could feel her presence." the voice said, and I gave her back to the world so swiftly that she slid from Laban's arms and collapsed in a glorious heap onto the floor.

Chapter Thirty-Seven

I N THE FORE DAY AS the music halted and the tired dancers drifted off the dance floor, across the yard where neighbours kept chickens a cock gave its full clarion. It was her new dawn's clarion call. Leaving the dance hall, some influence had held my hand fast and drawn me to her bed side. I was not the only one there; the aunts and the uncles were there, too. How could someone so blessed ever die alone?

After so many years, she did not mind going because she had made peace with her anointing; and had settled the matter of her descendants once and for all; for all to see where her thoughts were. They were with the first beginning before the beginning. Hence, the Book of Beheshti as it was from the beginning before the beginning. In the final few days of her life, it was clear that she had reverted to the teaching of her father Abraham, and that her heart was with the prophet Elias.

Even at that time of the morning the telephone lines were busy. The international calls rang like automated church bells. There were calls across the globe, and some in speaking said they had felt an inclination, a presence, a vibration in the air because where they were the sun had shone satin throughout the day, while the moon had hung like an orb of yellow satin in the twilight sky. Some even said the sun shone passed midnight. They had seen signs and wonders of signs. When Martha passed over it was a blessed day: she gave up the spirit and died. She was four score years and ten with one extra year for grace.

It did not matter in which of our homes you ate. The kitchen was familiar. There were always a large, polished mahogany dining table laden like a donkey with a crook of fruits. Chairs set around this table, in expectation of a feast. It was always as if they even expected the dearly departed to feel comfortable should their spirits return to visit living relatives.

They were seated around these tables in their respective homes. In mourning, but also planning the send-off, because to many people saw Martha's demise as a send over; like a cricketer at the crease, she had scored a near century and, had produced at least three full teams to carry on the game of life.

Three days had passed. There were mourning; there were tears. Then we were all gathered under one roof. The church had hanging lamp shades bright as orbs, the rostrum was polished mahogany - our familiar wood. In the middle, just before reaching the rostrum the cortege sat - bright mahogany - surrounded by flowers. The choir stood in the wings, either side.

The rendition began with pastor Dingle. This time, he surprised his congregation. It was direct and to the point. Then the hymns began and ended. Three of the young people with violin, cello, and the kora, played "Swing Low Sweet Chariot." In the grand multitude that seemed a great rehearsal for resurrection morning, my eyes swam the sea of faces to recognize those present, and those that were absent.

The final gift of our Martha was love, infinite love - unconditional - love, in all its glory, wonderment and splendour. We had in her rising and her waking a life lived for others, and for good. Renditions spoke of her patience, humility. Her exemplary acts of kindness; her wisdom; her tactful qualities. And I began to miss the world of the living and waxed afraid that someone near to passing over in that sacred place might see me in the multitude of the living or smell my offensive burning calamity; and fearing also that having again tasted the pleasures of life, that my heart would want to stay. So, I would linger on the plane of days indefinitely. It was then I asked for mercy to return my soul to Nadarina to await judgement.

So, I left them in the church while I could hear their singing. I fought hard to let go of the thrill of their sweet voices that rose in songs up to heaven, filled the air, circling the place where life, love and death exist in delicate balance, so cyclical and interlinked and which, greater love of God and our peculiar covenants with her; him or it, have been made indistinguishable. I asked God to put my spirit to rest and she answered my prayer.

Chapter Thirty-Eight

"DO YOU REMEMBER THE HOUSE in Waterston?" I was Cherry Blossom, then, the girl with the most winsome smile; those days were filled with bright days of our youth. You might recall the village strung between Kingswinford and Wolverhampton. We lived in so many houses: Handsworth, Greet, Sutton Coldfield. Yet, all had vanished as we were poor actors on the stage of life; we fluffed our lines and our hearts sank and in time our props, and great drama ended. Memories immutable like the forms are the only things that do not fall apart.

We moved away, and the houses were left desolate. Rudy had moved into the main house and could not manage the rest. Jay who had always been restless joined the Royal Navy soon after, and became intoxicated with the sea and exotic places, and rarely came home on leave. When his parents died both Rudy and Linda's children inherited the Morrison's home, and with the death of his uncle Rudy also took control of the Solomon's home next door.

This would have been given to Charlotte and Geremel, but they chose the Greet house instead, and when Rudy started drinking and Charlotte became estranged, Geremel lost all sense of purpose and joined him in his favourite pass time, so both properties eventually fell into the hands of Jay after Linda and her first daughter had drowned in that terrible boating tragedy in Australia. Rudy became fed up with life drank like a fish. He ran a second - hand business selling bottles, dressing tables, clocks, and mirrors with surplus stocks that he stored in the house. In the middle years I lived in Sheffield and had lost contact with the rest of the family. Having become successful people, first narrator and I spent much of our time travelling the air; two lost and disjointed spirits caught up in a whirlwind, between one place and another, desperate for an abiding place.

The Morrison's part of the property had been squatted by drunkards over the years, and it was left dilapidated and in need of major repairs, and we haunted the squatters, setting fire to their fears, until we drove them away: tearful, because of sleepless nights, traumatized because of floating objects and loud music for which they could give no logical reasons, or account for.

As to our courtship, he wanted me. He always wanted me - even as children he found me hard to resist, and I knew I had caught him. That afternoon asleep in his bed, my soul had taken flight and was hovering over some river or waterway in the world, I knew not where, but my heart had been sacrificed in the body of a crocodile, in a lake that is linked to the stars.

That afternoon when he came for me, I had found a great gaping hole in the ground where he would later build a time capsule for our story. This was not the first time we had buried accounts of our lives. King Jaja was the one who would normally bury objects in the back yard. He had only recently buried his ginger and bottles filled with his special potions, which he called bitters and marked each one according to year, type, and strength. I was thrilled and excited to see what the earth had made of the green bottles, especially, after reading about the benefits of rum-based medicines. I had seen the first distilled liquor of the time capsule that he had buried, and which has been excavated round the back of the large, sprawling, and dilapidated property in which Iron Sound was housed, and which we called the outhouse.

I always knew I had allure, for I was born with a caul. And these black arts protected me from evil, and realizing my power, I went to look at the handiwork of King Jaja, and so following on from that I went to sleep all excited, and slept like a child, without a care in the world. And my soul took flight above the Abrodwum Stone in the middle of the lake, whilst first voice was the man in the padua fishing in the upstream, on the sacred lake where only wooden boats and can sail. I was gone, forever, lost in a reverie.

And, as Solomon wrote, ""I sought my beloved, and my bowels moved for him""" - meaning I had butterflies. In our case the consanguineous, though, consensual congress of our father Abraham, and his sister Sarah, has left an indelible mark on us, for their sins have visited the fourth and the fifth generations; and they in turn have passed on this stain unto the twelfth generation and the end of time. But who decides when time began, and where time ends?

But unlike other restless, and furtive spirits, we are goodly angels: we wear our masks; have neither numbers, nor horns on our foreheads, but they are implants under our skin; our flaws are plain for all to see. But we never change. We are content with mediocrity. To distinguish us from the sprites of Satan. We are God's good spirits, where goodness is a sin. Primordial, colourless as slime. We have conscience. Lest our betrayal is in the skin: the weakest human stain. Therefore, conscience is the grey, and seminal matter of our brain, for our gift is at once spiritual and physical - a metaphysical love: supreme, far beyond compare. Yet fragile and inconsequential. We build no heaven on earth but wait patiently for our demise to achieve it.

They all saw this in Henrietta's capitulation to Geremel, and even Aunty Bertha had seen it, and had even encouraged it, and had even remarked why my eyes followed Joseph as a young girl, and as a woman. She had even tricked me with perfumes to sleep in his bed that afternoon when his strength was at a low ebb, with his newly arrived home from work.

Consanguineous love is endemic to the tapestries of our history, and crochet - patented into the very nature of our being, and the fight begins and ends within from the inner side. The battle of good or ill, is the struggle from within. The environments, both within and without have made us Levy, and Solomon split, like a cutlass to a coconut to reveal, sometimes, the slightly hard meat, but we are the young, green coconut, with its soft, jelly - like slime; with its pure, medicinal water that washes the heart. Yet we have no permanence, neither in this life nor the next.

Chapter Thirty-Nine

THAT WAS THE LAST TIME I saw her. I saw her. She broke my heart and made me lose my mind. (Siobhan, you should never have done that to me, to us!) I loved you; we loved you beyond words. She could not have been more than thirty metres away when I saw her on the bridge over the road leading to the motor way, a beautiful, young, girl child, and of course, I recognized her immediately, it was young Siobhan, my god child and Rudy's daughter.

Our girl of white socks and white petty coats climbed through the railings, her skirt flying and flapping in the wind; unbelieving I watched her; we watched her horrified and helpless we were, even as she smoothed her hair back, and cupped her face in her hands and jumped, and I gulped as if my heart had stopped and came out through my mouth.

Over the motor way she hovered like a giant bird strapped to a boxer kite, then, plunged feet first into the traffic below. The screeching tyres of halted cars and other vehicles and the impact shook the air so that the air seemed to tremble for miles around from that sudden thud; there was a sudden hush. A deafening silence. It felt as if a tsunami had washed over the whole universe, and, drowned all the nations.

The pause lingered in slow motion; then the world sped up. The well of silence broken as came the police cars and ambulances: their sirens like curlews crying, tolling, and chilling, as they raced to another of our blood spilt spots. I wrung my hands and cried the question, why did we ever come here?

"Lawd," I said, "Why did we ever come to this terrible place?" And a part of me died with that child and I vowed, then, to go home to glory, and take my children with me because a living death is unbearable. What was more puzzling, Geremel turned up. There will be comfort in numbers, and we were, terrible as nihilism may seem, all in it together.

As night fell, I was thankful; we were thankful for the conflagration when after consuming three bottles of rum alone. Crates of which they had dug from the time capsules over the years - and after drinking a flask with us, he set fire to the house and we were oh, so grateful for the end of the pain that we did not rush out; we did not scream; we did not run out. We held hands in a circle of six as our souls prepared to say farewell to life, finding that gap within the gloaming to hold briefly in the imagination, as if almost in actual sight, nine days and nine nights lit by a golden satin sun, and a purple satin moon in a southern sky emblazoned with glory where souls hover above the sacred lake to say farewell to the earth before the body dies, and the soul flies through a red satin crack through the ceiling to enter the black hole within the gloaming. Ours is a universe of nothingness. And so, we stood in the warehouse of his house where thirty or so dressing cabinets stood huddled against the partition.

Then the majestic rivers; crack of gold in the twilight opened. The beauty captured my heart and soul; and my heart, but especially, my soul flew like a bird above satin lakes and streams of cool, clear, crystal waters; the estuaries of the Milky Way River turning to liquid gold. And my spirit flew through streets, beaten with leaves of gold, paved with jewels and precious stones, a place unlike no other place on earth where the souls go back. The newly arisen soul clothed in the brightest of light, soared above the new city of walls, pillars and crystals that shone brighter than the shattered and reflecting mirrors in the storeroom of the family home.

The straight and narrow pathways bordered with rose petals, strewn with diamonds, beryl, and onyx, stretched before me. The twelve golden stairways opened, and I beheld the glory of my resurrection.

In this my ascendance from the pit of chaos. I exhaled my last breath and thought about my first footsteps down the plank; snow rising with the gusts of wind that blasted my face. Snowflakes falling from the sky; blue seagulls screeching, squawking, and whinnying over our heads, some landing on the rocks.

This was our world: the sea. But once again, I had been hallucinating. Hallucinations have become the fabric of our existence where we have died as voices over the sea. Realise that nothing I say now or have ever said to you was ever real. Descendants of the sea, we are delusional by birth.

Suddenly, a flash; it came back to me in that last flash moment, as it does in all our lives, that our beliefs have been futile; all we held tied to neck chains as we sought salvation in our own oppression by subconscious acceptance of the zeitgeist in which we served as secondary souls. Where more intelligent minds would have cultivated a consensus for disambiguation from our conquerors. But we live in hope and die in hope for the resurrection, I might say that having lived so many lives. But that was not my eventual end.

Chapter Forty

SUMMONED TO REMOVE THE DEAD. Summoned to replace and bury the dead and to protect the living from the zombies of the past. The walking dead that are uninstructed shall be buried, not by water as at the time of Noah with his boat that was filled with fear. In the new Armageddon, the fire next time. Ancestral explosions shall light the new fires of jihad. We shall gather at their doors like the stampede of elephants, we who have no states; we who have no nations, for we must return to the sources of our effluence. But we are like grains of sand at the bottom of the sea.

This brings me to my dreams of hope, like so many before me taken away by the machinations of war, I must find myself through all the lives that I have lived because I am housed inside a shell that craves, that functions because of waste, that craves for love and zin, all the unspiritual things that make the senses bearable. This body is a tent in which we reside. It is like paradise: a punishment. All else is delusion. On my trips to the islands, I have witnessed the punishment of paradise.

During the outbreak of the breaking up of faith, I saw Chaguaramas bleed. In Kingston, I watched the rat pellets in the sugar. And across the cowrie - chain of islands, mice ate chewing like squirrels in the warehouses' mountains of sugar.

In Bridgetown one day, I saw a man on the tall ship built for tourists and called "The Jolly Roger." He sang the shanty 'Sally Brown'. The thrills of the banjo sweetening the sexual slavery of this mulatto woman that reminded me so much of Nana that I felt violent. But that is the reality of their voices over the sea. We were a broken people. Newly healed, and not destroyed, but here! We are here! Mwe la! (I am here!)

It was a hot spring day when I arrived at the new home at Waterson View (as it has been rechristened). In my invisible form I saw the two houses standing opposite each other; now occupied by the new people. Three children: two girls and a boy were chasing one another across the lawns to the steps of the one house, and when they got to the other house they turned and raced back. I saw them there at last, a different type of people, pale and a lighter shade of pale. These were our new descendants, lighter and still lithe of limbs. And it did not matter that they looked white. They raced across the lawns nonchalant, innocent, and unselfconscious. Impartial and indestructible, changeable as matter mutates. But not destroyed. "Who can destroy us? What principalities? What powers? Who can destroy the beginning?"

There was war in heaven.

Yes, reader, as I wrote, the Gods Yemaya, Onyankopong, and Obatala caught in the cyclone, spoke these words. Yemaya possessed first voice, shimmering in bark cloth, adorned with cowries, freshly arrived from his war with Ulunkulu in the southern heaven.

"My brothers, there is nothing to destroy us, simply because we are already destroyed. We do not speak our languages; we celebrate the zeitgeists of the double - conquerors. We alone of all peoples join the celebrations of the conquerors over us, and the ones that vanquished our innocent ancestors. Look for example in the descendants of Chineke. In them are the conquerors glorified, and their God Jesus triumphs in his destruction of our destroyers, and his rule over us."

"Well, it appears that you are right" replied Obatala, removing his crown of mimosa from his head, "there are principalities and powers that have dictated to us. Whole armies that have destroyed our right to our own destiny. Indeed, we have no power to confront the dark and secretive mischiefs that until now, despite so many wars, with so many lives lost (on both sides) the conquerors hold fast to our heels like crazed Jacob to his own ankles thinking that they were the bronze feet of God."

Onyankopong, fixed his Kente on his shoulder and laughed, pounding his chest with a clenched fist. "You blaspheme, my brother". But quickly corrected himself. "But we are Gods, so how shall we blaspheme?"

Suddenly, a fireball appeared in the cyclone, out of which spun a hurricane and a typhoon. There was an explosion and a flash of fire. And in the engulfing smoke Ghede, who was the hurricane appeared with a rocket on his head. There was room made for him in the throne made of Colton and gold. He was followed by the typhoon, out of which stepped Onyankotron wearing two horns in the middle of which was a disk for the moon. They offered a throne, but she refused, preferring to stand.

Ghede waved his right hand decorated with precious gems and medals. "Our conquerors were with us. The God that is the cosmos made it so that the nations of the earth were all good. They had the greatest dispensations that ever were given to the human being. The opportunity to build the Aquarius of justice in its purity to the world. But they took their blessedness to conquer; to usurp; to rape the world."

Onyankotron looked at her polished fingernails, looked down at her polished toenails, but said nothing. The men alarmed at her silence looked at her but kept the peace and waited patiently.

Then she spoke: "They were with us, Allah had blest them with us. They have failed to keep the peace, and they have failed themselves. They did not listen enough to their better angels. And where did they fail? 'As you sow, so shall you reap. The arrogance of hubris was their default. But look how like the sea we all are? All of us are evil and good. And like the sea: calm, tumultuous, predictable, unpredictable. Strong but still moved by the moon, unusually calm before the storm. Constantly changing and destructive; positively good as well as evil. In a constant stasis of change. Like the sea.'

That is all well and good. But I am Abiku; I am Horus, the avenging child. Men that broker peace and inflict themselves, imposing their truths upon me, have wedged a gulf between us. But I am bringer of the storm. The unforgiving souls drowned at the bottom of lakes in America. The twitching limbs burned on trees. In me entwined are all the souls the souls of naked men, women and children stripped bare of their shame on the auction blocks. I do not forgive. For even in their books, it has been prophesied that the sins of the fathers shall visit unto the sixth generation. And if that is so, just as I know no peace today. Tomorrow my enemies shall not know peace. For I shall strike; strike relentless and bloody at the throats of my enemies. Awaken the storm to wage wars until all fortresses that are arrayed against me fall. Destined as we are to destruction for that day in 2050, when the sun shall be darkened, and the moon shall turn into blood.

Yet I do not; cannot recoil from the coals of fire; this oblique future; for I am become fickle. Do you condone what manner of soul, I have become?'